Other Bells for Us to Ring

Other Bells for Us to Ring

Robert Cormier

Illustrated by Deborah Kogan Ray

Delacorte Press

Published by
Delacorte Press
Bantam Doubleday Dell Publishing Group, Inc.
666 Fifth Avenue
New York, New York 10103

Library of Congress Cataloging in Publication Data

Cormier, Robert.
    Other bells for us to ring / by Robert Cormier ; illustrated by
Deborah Kogan Ray.
        p.   cm.
    Summary: When her father is transferred to an army camp in
Massachusetts during the Second World War, Darcy feels isolated
in her French-Canadian neighborhood until she meets the
vivacious Kathleen Mary O'Hara and learns about Catholicism.
    ISBN 0-385-30245-2
    [1. Catholics—Fiction.   2. Friendship—Fiction.   3. World War,
1939–1945—United States—Fiction.]   I. Ray, Deborah Kogan,
1940– , ill. II. Title.
PZ7.C816340t   1990
[Fic]—dc20   90-3326
                                                                 CIP
                                                                  AC

Manufactured in the United States of America
November 1990
10 9 8 7 6 5 4 3 2 1
RRH

To the New Generation:
Jennifer, Travis, Darren,
Emily, Mallory, and Claire

And to the memory
of
Hazel Tedford Heald,
who also was sprinkled with holy water
a long time ago

AT THE NEW YEAR

In the shape of this night, in the still fall
      of snow, Father
In all that is cold and tiny, these little birds
      and children
In everything that moves tonight, the trolleys
      and the lovers, Father
In the great hush of country, in the ugly noise
      of our cities
In this deep throw of stars, in those trenches
      where the dead are, Father
In all the wide land waiting, and in the liners
      out on the black water
In all that has been said bravely, in all that is
      mean anywhere in the world, Father
In all that is good and lovely, in every house
      where sham and hatred are
In the name of those who wait, in the sound
      of angry voices, Father
Before the bells ring, before this little point
      in time has rushed us on
Before this clean moment has gone, before this
      night turns to face tomorrow, Father
There is this high singing in the air
Forever this sorrowful human face in
      eternity's window
And there are other bells that we would ring,
      Father
Other bells that we would ring.

KENNETH PATCHEN

*E*verybody in those days was singing "Praise the Lord and Pass the Ammunition" and "Mairzy Doats" to keep their spirits up because the war was still going on and our soldiers were fighting all over Europe and in places like Guadalcanal in the South Pacific, and here at home you needed ration stamps to buy meat and even shoes, and little children saved up money to buy U.S. War Bonds. That was also the year we moved to Frenchtown in a lonesome place called Monument near Fort Delta in Massachusetts where Kathleen Mary O'Hara altered the events of my life when she sprinkled me with holy water in the vestibule of St. Brendan's Church and pronounced those terrible words:

"Now you're a Catholic, Darcy Webster. Forever and ever, world without end, Amen."

Me a Catholic?

My mother and father and I attended the Unitarian Church, when we could find such a place in our travels. "Unitarians," my father always said, "are the Protestants of the Protestants. We barely acknowledge the existence of God."

"Speak for yourself, William Webster," my mother said, pretending to be shocked, although I doubt that my father could ever shock her. She was always gentle with him, even when he announced after we had lived in a new place for only a few months, that we were moving again. He didn't exactly make an announcement but stood with his hat in his hand, like a small boy asking permission to go to the bathroom, and my mother would sigh and fan herself with her damp apron and finally nod in acceptance, a resigned smile on her face.

Our travels were necessary, my father had said, because a man had to search for work back in those Depression days, although he admitted, somewhat sheepishly, that he was touched with wanderlust. "Itchy feet," my mother called it. But it was not wanderlust or itchy feet that brought us to

Massachusetts. The reason we came hung in the closet of our latest tenement in Frenchtown, the uniform of an enlisted man in the United States Army.

"A man has to do his duty for his country," he said the day he came home and announced that he had joined the army. This was in Clapham, North Carolina, and the next thing you knew we were riding in a train to Fort Delta, where he was assigned after completing his basic training.

As we stood on the second-floor porch of the three-decker on Second Street, looking out at the landscape of tenement houses and clotheslines and the steeples of St. Jude's Church, my mother said, "Know what you've done this time, William?"

"What have I done, Abby?" my father asked. He had a way of putting a smile in his voice on occasion.

"You've put us smack in the middle of a French-Canadian neighborhood. Roman Catholic too."

"There was a G.I. in basic who came from here. He told me it was a good place to live when he heard I was transferred to Delta. Come to think of it, he was a Frenchman and a Catholic. Called himself the Fighting Canuck, but I never saw him fight."

What's a Canuck, I wondered.

"William, William," my mother said, scolding but tender as he came and stood beside her, "what am I going to do with you?"

3

"I have a suggestion or two," he said, placing his arm around her waist and pulling her toward him.

I turned away because it embarrassed me when my father kissed my mother or embraced her or ran his hand across her body. She always made a joke of it, evading him in a flirting way. "There's a time and a place for everything, William," she'd admonish. And he always answered, "I've got the time if you've got the place."

Although these scenes made my cheeks burn, the gentle joking that went on between them, as if they shared a secret from the rest of the world, made me feel safe and secure. They made up for the times when my father became remote, present with us in whatever place we were living but somehow not really *with* us. He'd be sitting with my mother and me at the kitchen table or listening to the radio but separate and alone at the same time. He was sad, I thought. But I knew that *sad* was not the right word.

"Well, we'll make the best of it," my mother said now, evading my father's hands and bustling into the house, beckoning me to follow. "Come on, Darcy. Let's put this place in order."

My mother loved order and neatness and everything in its place and daisies in glass vases on windowsills, and made the best of it whenever we moved. But I hated moving, packing all my

4

possessions once more and leaving my friends behind.

Wait a minute—I am lying ferociously now. I never had *that* many possessions, mostly my books— *Anne of Green Gables* and *Anne of Avonlea* and *Little Women* and my Shirley Temple doll along with the Shirley Temple paper dolls and my Little Orphan Annie mug, which had a crack down its side and was yellow with age now.

I had no real friends at all, only acquaintances, girls who might have become my friends if we'd lived in one place long enough.

Hold the phone. I am lying again. And also engaging in self-pity. The truth is that most of the time I did not make friends because I didn't try. I was too shy, did not know what to say when meeting strangers, did not know what to do with my hands, did not know how to stand properly, my body awkward. But I was not awkward with Shirley Temple, and held long conversations with her, and my books presented a world more wonderful than anyplace we ever lived.

Later that evening my father appeared in the kitchen in his uniform, the neatly pressed suntan trousers and shirt, the beige tie tucked crisply into the khaki shirt between the third and fourth buttons, his cap on his head at a devil-may-care angle. He was handsome and dashing like a movie star. But Hollywood stars did not get killed in the movies. Only real people did. And my father was real.

I kept smiling anyway, although it hurt my cheeks.

The next day I met Kathleen Mary O'Hara.

She came out of nowhere, planting herself in front of me across the street from Lucier's Meat Market, where my mother had dispatched me with a grocery list and a pocketbook full of ration stamps.

With her orange hair and flashing green eyes, she seemed to inhabit a Technicolor movie, while I was still in black and white.

"You're new here, aren't you," she declared, a question mark absent from her voice.

"Yes," I said, the shame of shyness burning in my cheeks.

"My name is Kathleen Mary O'Hara," she said, "what's yours?" Not asking but demanding.

"Darcy Webster." How many times had I supplied that information in a new neighborhood?

"Webster," she mused, rolling those green eyes, grimacing, her freckles dancing on her cheeks.

"That's Protestant, isn't it?" Looking directly at me now, accusingly.

"That's right," I said, planting my own feet firmly, preparing myself for an assault of some kind. Maybe an ambush by someone crouching around the corner, her brother, perhaps—if she had one— waiting to pounce at her signal.

"I never met a Protestant before," she said.

"Well, I never met a Catholic before," I said, standing my ground, but not certain whether I had ever met one or not. "I assume you are a Catholic." *Assume:* one of my favorite words, which I seldom had a chance to use.

"Oh, I'm Catholic, all right," she said. "But I'm an outsider here, just like you. Me, I'm Irish, a Mick. But you, even worse, are a Yankee and a Protestant. The two of us here in the land of the Canucks."

"The what?"

"The Canucks," she said. "That's what they call the Frenchies, the French Canadians." She gestured with her left hand. "Next door to Frenchtown is the Vines, where the Eyeties grow their grapes for the wine." Seeing my frown, she explained as if talking to a second-grader: "Eyeties are Italians." She pronounced it "Eye-talians." "What a bunch we are here in the United States of America—Micks and Canucks and Eyeties, to say nothing of colored people and Yankees and Jews too. And we're all fighting for the cause of freedom." Her voice rang like a bell, and it was difficult to tell whether she was being sarcastic or sincere.

This was the first speech I heard Kathleen Mary O'Hara make. I soon found out that she liked explaining things and making speeches about almost any subject without even a minute's notice.

She leaned toward me confidentially:

"Know what we've got to do, Darcy Webster?" Her orange hair was on fire in the sunlight.

"What?" I asked, astonished at becoming a conspirator with Kathleen Mary O'Hara.

"Stick together, that's what," she said. "Know that poem?"

"What poem?" I asked, dazzled at the twists and turns of this amazing conversation.

" 'The Man with the Hoe,' by Edwin Markham." She stood at attention as if on a stage and in a deep voice, recited:

"Bowed by the weight of centuries he leans . . ."

I leapt in, remembering the poem from English, my best subject, in Miss Margaret Robinson's class in Holliston, Alabama: *"Upon his hoe and gazes at the ground . . ."*

Kathleen Mary O'Hara's eyes flashed like emeralds as she picked up the pace: *"The emptiness of ages in his face . . ."*

I added, *"And on his back the burden of the world."*

We gazed at each other in wonder and delight, silent for a moment in joyful recognition.

"But that's not the poem I mean," she said.

Instantly deflated, I sighed and turned to leave, clutching my pocketbook with the ration stamps that my mother said were more precious than jewels.

"Wait," she said, touching my shoulder. "There's another poem by Edwin Markham—that's the important one." Lowering her voice again, she said, "It will be our credo."

Credo. A word that made bells ring. I prayed to my Protestant God, the God of my father's Unitarian Church, that I would also know this poem that Kathleen Mary O'Hara had declared as our credo, our code, words to live by.

She closed her eyes, threw her head back, which made her orange hair bristle, and intoned,

> *"He drew a circle that left me out*
> *Heretic, rebel, a thing to flout . . ."*

Again, my heart soared in recognition, and I finished the poem in a voice bright with hope and valor:

> *"But love and I had the wit to win,*
> *We drew a circle that took him in!"*

9

"Wow," Kathleen Mary exclaimed, her voice like a flag flying over a field of battle. "Only, it's not *him* but *them*, that we shut out. You and me against the Canucks, the Micks, everybody in the whole wide world. Including the Japs and the Nazis. You and me, Darcy Webster."

I knew I had found a best friend at last.

Kathleen Mary O'Hara lived in a three-decker on Ninth Street that was identical to my own three-decker on Second Street, both houses painted gray. We found shortcuts so we could reach our houses without wasting time. Drawn together against enemies that did not really exist—the boys and girls of Frenchtown ignored us most of the time while the Japs and Nazis did not know of our presence on the earth—we spent most of our free time together.

We were eleven years old, conscious of the terrible realities of being eleven. Eleven was a nothing time, not one thing or another, no longer a child and certainly not a woman and not even a teenager. Eleven was a season of its own, a pause between spring and summer. Boys hated eleven-year-old girls, and we hated them back. Kathleen Mary fought constantly with her brothers, the three who were still at home, that is. (Three others were in the service of their country.)

As best friends we had much in common, and much not in common. We both loved poetry, the kind we learned in school, although we went to different schools—"If" by Rudyard Kipling and "Sunset and evening star and one clear call for me" and especially "I have been faithful to thee, Cynara, in my fashion," reciting the lines to each other. But Kathleen Mary also read *True Confessions* and the romances in the ten-cent magazines from the drugstore. I had embarked on reading all of the Green Gables books, delighted to discover at the Monument Public Library that their author, Lucy Montgomery, had written an entire series of other books about girls growing up on Prince Edward Island.

Kathleen Mary and I also dressed differently, but it did not affect our friendship. She wore pants and boys' shirts handed down from her brothers, while my mother insisted that I wear skirts or dresses like a lady and used a curling iron on my hair. Kathleen Mary's bristling hair did not need a brush or curler but remained fiery and in place even when she ran. I admired the way she scrambled up fences and climbed trees and never scratched herself or broke any bones or sprained her ankles. I did not break any bones, simply because I did not follow Kathleen

Mary in her exploits. Although a willing companion, I was content to read a book while she sat on a fence, spying on her brothers, who were sneaking smokes in back of Laurier's Drugstore, hooting at them, promising to squeal on them unless they paid her a penny for every cigarette they smoked. They never paid and she never squealed.

Actually we did not spend as much time together as best friends should. She attended St. Brendan's Parochial School on Main Street downtown, while I went to Mechanic Street Public School a few blocks away from my house. The French-Canadian kids attended St. Jude's Parochial School, next to the church. After school Kathleen Mary was kept busy with chores at her house, helping her mother, a woman of vague gestures who always seemed lost in thought. Kathleen Mary cooked and cleaned the tenement. "I'm eleven years old and already fed up with housework," she said. "I may become a nun. Or kill myself by sixteen." She said this with a glint in her eye, however. I was certain that Kathleen Mary would never kill herself. Become a nun? I did not consider that a possibility either. Whenever I passed by St. Jude's Convent, a tall, secretive building surrounded by a maze of shrubbery, I pictured long, dark corridors inside and women enveloped in black and white whispering to each other while candles burned. I could not imagine Kathleen Mary in such a place.

I had my own chores in our tenement, particularly when my mother was besieged by headaches that sent her to bed with the shades drawn while I brought wet towels and placed them on her forehead. She was small and delicate, like a ballet dancer. When she walked, her feet almost didn't touch the floor. She did not believe in sitting still, but kept busy cleaning, washing, ironing. She knitted, she made quilts. At the sewing machine she made most of my dresses as well as miniature versions of those same dresses for my Shirley Temple doll.

When I confessed to Kathleen Mary that the doll was one of my prized possessions, she looked disgusted. "Shirley Temple's now a teenager," she said. "How come you're still playing with a doll, anyway?"

Stung by her remark, I made no reply.

She squinted at me and ran her hand through her hair and shook her head. "Okay, I'm sorry," she said. She reached out and brushed a lock of my hair away from my face. "Know what? I still wear my Jane Withers hat sometimes, even though she's all grown up, too, like Shirley Temple."

Kathleen Mary drew me away from Shirley

Temple and my paper dolls and books and took me on explorations of Frenchtown. We strolled through the tumult of Third Street with its assortment of stores, ducking past people holding bags of groceries and women wheeling baby carriages.

Men swaggered in front of the Welcome Bar, their thumbs hooked into their belts. Soldiers and sailors strolled the sidewalk, khaki and navy blue the colors of wartime America. Occasional cars chugged by: gasoline was in short supply, and no new cars were emerging from the factories, only guns and tanks and other equipment for our fighting men and women. We were wonderful lingerers on that busy street. We lingered outside Madame Chapdeleine's Boston Confectionery Store, inhaling the sweet mixture of chocolate and caramel and peppermint. We sneaked into Lucier's Market and inspected the fish counter, where mackerels, packed in ice, stared at us with deadly eyes, giving us chills. Mr. Lucier was generous with lollipops and did not mind having us hang around. We always tingled with apprehension as we peeked into Henry Ling's Chinese Laundry, wide-eyed and curious as the thin, sunken-cheeked man, a cigarette permanently dangling from his lips, ironed shirts and handkerchiefs. "What a mixed-up Chinaman he must be, running a laundry in Canuckville," Kathleen

Mary whispered as we waited for the ash from his cigarette to fall on a clean white shirt. He always caught the ash in a cupped hand at the last possible moment, and we raced away.

After our visits we stopped at the edge of Moosock Brook, which went underground at Fourth Street and emerged at the end of a tunnel near Ninth. Boys hung around the tunnel, doing whatever boys do, and sometimes they saw us and hooted. Boys, in fact, seemed to be everywhere in Frenchtown, especially on street corners, and they either yelled boisterously at us or ignored us altogether. They did not flirt or whistle at our female attributes—which, of course, were nonexistent. They hurled insults—freckle-face, skinny, four-eyes—and we ran away from them. Sometimes Kathleen Mary would stop at a safe distance, turn and face the boys, stick out her tongue, cross her eyes and hurl insults back at them, repeating words she'd learned from her brothers—*scum of the earth, stupid Canucks, sons of bitches*—that made me squirm and blush. Then we'd hurry down the street, Kathleen Mary's hair blazing brightly and a satisfied smirk on her face: "That'll show the bastards."

Four-eyes. Those were the words that wounded me. The tragedy of my life was that I wore glasses, steel-rimmed, ugly glasses that magnified my eyes so that they looked like those mackerel eyes in Lucier's Market. I hated them, but it was impossible for me to read a blackboard or see across the street without them. "You have a wonderful complexion, peaches and cream," my mother said, "People won't even notice your glasses." But they did. I know *I* did when I encountered my reflection, without warning, in a store window or an unexpected mirror. The glasses kept slipping down my nose, and my mother always reminded me to push them up. They were easily smudged, and I wiped them on the hem of my skirt, which irritated my mother.

I held my head at an awkward angle when I ran because they had a tendency to fall off if I bent my head a certain way. Sometimes one of the lenses shattered when the glasses fell off, and I spent two or three wonderful days while they were being repaired, gazing longingly at myself in the mirror, although to tell the truth the absence of glasses did not turn me into a sudden beauty. I hated the movies in which a plain girl with glasses would become a ravishing beauty when she removed them and the fellow who had ignored her until that moment fell instantly in love with her. The absence of freckles was my only physical virtue. "I hate my freckles," Kathleen Mary said. But her orange hair was a luminous halo around her head, while my hair was

16

thick and heavy, without any luster, and it brushed my cheeks annoyingly when I ran or bent my head over my desk at school.

———❖❖❖———

My father loved my long black hair and protested when my mother sometimes braided it. He stroked my hair as we listened to the New York Philharmonic on the radio on Sunday afternoons. He loved music of all kinds, jazz and symphony, crazy songs like "Mairzy Doats," which he sang softly like a lullaby when he tucked me into bed. "Only reason your father ever went to church was to hear the organ," my mother said in that joking way she had with him.

Glancing at him occasionally as we sat one afternoon listening to the music on the radio, I pondered the secret of his sadness and realized that he was not exactly sad. What then? He was—wistful. Yes, that was the mood. Wistful, a lonely country on the border of sadness. I found out the secret of his wistfulness one day in Tarbox, Maine, when I discovered the small box carefully hidden in the cellar of the house we rented there.

The box had first caught my attention years

*Yes, that was the mood. A lonely country on the border of
sadness.*

before because we took it with us whenever we moved. We did not pack it away with our belongings; either my mother or my father carried it. On that Sunday afternoon in Tarbox, bored and restless in a town that held no attraction for me, not even a movie house, and most of my schoolmates living outside of town in the farmlands, I wandered to the cellar, my feet scuffling across the dirt floor, the smell of last year's apples musty in the air. I inspected the decrepit furniture abandoned by the previous tenants. In an ancient, dusty cupboard, behind a clutter of junk, I spotted my father's mysterious package, wrapped in brown paper, tied with store string. Clever at undoing knots and happy for a task to end my boredom, I carefully opened the package and took out a bottle of whiskey wrapped in an old newspaper. A brown bottle, *Seagram's 7* on the label.

I couldn't imagine why my father took this package with him all over the country. Why didn't he simply drink the whiskey? I had never seen him drink whiskey or beer, however. He drank coffee at breakfast and sometimes tea at suppertime.

Footsteps on the cellar stairs made me leap with guilt, and I turned to see my mother looking down at me. "That's not a nice thing to do, Darcy," she said, kneading her forehead, the old sign of a headache, as if she could pluck the pain from her head. "Put it back just as you found it. Carefully. And I'll tell you the story of that bottle."

We finished at the same time, the story and the wrapping, and I knew finally the answer to puzzling events I had tucked away in a corner of my mind. For instance the men who came to the house on occasion through the years and sat up with my father while my mother and I went to bed. How I'd hear the men murmur strange phrases like, "One more hour, Bill, one more hour." Or "easy does it" or "one day at a time." Repeating the phrases over and over, and only silence from my father. Once in a while my father went to "meetings," and something in his manner kept me from asking what kind of meetings. For a while I thought he was a spy or a secret agent and that that was why we traveled so much. In that Tarbox cellar my mother told me that my father was a drinker and would always be a drinker, even though alcohol had not touched his lips since the day of my birth.

"He vowed at my bedside, the first time he held you in his arms, that he would never touch another drop," my mother said. "And he never has. The thirst is always with him, though. He gets tempted, especially when things go wrong, and then he needs help. The people at AA help him—Alcoholics Anonymous," she explained when she saw the question in my eyes. "Do you know what it's like to have a burning desire all the time and you can never satisfy yourself? That's what being a drinker is."

"But why does he keep the bottle in the house?" I asked.

"We all have our tricks for getting by," she said. "And your father's trick is the bottle. He says that if he did not have a bottle nearby, then he would be in a panic and his thirst would be worse. But knowing it's here, knowing he could open it at any time, makes him feel better, takes away the panic. But he never opens it, Darcy."

"The same bottle, Mom, after all these years?"

"A lot of them," she said. "Some broke. One I dropped back in Clapham doing spring housecleaning. Another he dropped getting on a train. Now we keep it in a box, wrapped up in newspaper so that it won't break if we drop it."

She closed the door of the cupboard. "See how much he loves you, Darcy? It's easy to make a promise but hard to keep one. Unless there's a lot of love there."

Maybe he hates me, I thought in sudden panic. He gave up something he loves because of me. That doubt fled quickly when he came home from work that day, kissing my mother on the lips as he passed his hand across her buttocks and then turned to me and said, "And how's my girl today?" I did not see hate in his eyes.

Stars hung in many of the Frenchtown windows, as they did all over America, blue stars on white banners signifying that someone in the family was serving in the armed forces. A gold star meant that someone had died, most likely in battle, far from home.

I was proud of the blue star in our parlor window, but missed my father, although Fort Delta was only seventeen miles from Frenchtown. He seemed far away because he slept at the fort and did not come home very often.

The five-room tenement grew bigger when darkness fell outside and the lamps were turned on. Shadows were deeper, filling all the corners. When I woke up in the middle of the night, the sounds in the tenement were loud and terrifying. Night sounds had never bothered me before. In fact I had never awakened very much during the night. Now I woke up once or twice, eyes wide open, ears listening to dark noises—the faucet dripping, scurryings in the walls (mice?), a crackling in the kitchen linoleum (burglars?). My heart pounded, my body oozed perspiration as I curled up in the blankets, too scared to call to my mother or run to her bedroom next to mine.

My mother and I did not speak of my father's absence. I caught her looking out the window sometimes in the evening, holding the shade back with one hand so that she could see the street outside. Something forlorn in her posture. Occasionally, out of habit, she'd begin to set the table for three and then catch herself. She'd shake her head in dismay. But we wouldn't speak about it. Not even in a joking way. When I said my prayers at night, tucked in my bed, *Now I lay me down to sleep,* I added a special plea to God to keep my father safe in the army. I had always prayed for my father and mother and all the poor people of the world. Automatic prayers. Now that I tried to inject meaning into my prayers, I felt at a loss. How do you get God to listen to an eleven-year-old girl?

When my father came home from Fort Delta, always without advance notice, he would burst into the house in his uniform, hug my mother, and swing me into his arms, dashing in his uniform. Sometimes he stayed a few hours, sometimes overnight. "Let's splurge," my mother would say, and send me off to the store after checking her ration stamps. During my father's absences she was careful with them, purchasing food, such as canned corn or carrots, that required only six or seven stamps, but she spent them wildly when my father showed up, hoping that the stores would not be out of meat or butter.

He arrived one afternoon, swaggering a bit. Grinning, he displayed his right arm with the two stripes of a corporal on his sleeve. "I miss you both, but for once in my life, I'm doing work that I love," he said. He had been assigned to the corps of engineers and was learning to build and repair bridges. "Maybe after the war I can get a job on bridges and we can settle down, the three of us." His voice was so vibrant and hopeful that my throat constricted. I searched for wistfulness in his face and did not find any and wanted to shout hooray.

"Any news about shipping out?" my mother asked, trying to be casual, but her voice heartbreakingly bright and as fragile as glass. As the weeks of his training passed, my mother's big worry was that my father would be sent overseas where the fighting was going on. She began reading the newspapers thoroughly and listening to news broadcasts on the radio. The news remained vague and uninteresting to me. It was hard for me to care about events happening across the oceans, especially when my father was still in the United States.

My father always reassured my mother that there was little chance of his going overseas. "We've got enough bridge building to do right here at home," he said, "so that our troops can move around."

I did not believe that for a minute, and, from the expression on her face, I knew my mother did not either.

Kathleen Mary's father was not in the service. He was a big, roaring man, as loud and blustery as her mother was wispy and ethereal, her voice just above a whisper. Mr. O'Hara dragged his right leg as he walked, the result of a shop accident years ago. The injury and his large family—six sons and a daughter— kept him out of uniform. He drank huge quantities of beer that he brewed in his cellar. He did not sway down the street like other drinkers or fall into the gutter and sleep away his drunkenness on a bench in Monument Park. But always at some point in the drinking he became angry. Dark scowls crossed his face, and his eyes froze. Everybody fled the tenement as he raged through the rooms breaking furniture and dishes and throwing stuff out the windows.

"I love my father," Kathleen Mary said defiantly. "He works hard at the shop, on shifts now with war work." The shops of Monument operated twenty-four hours a day, producing products exclusively for our men in the armed services, combs and brushes and soap dishes and other utensils. The Viscoid Company was rumored to be manufacturing a secret component made out of a new material called Lucite for use in bombers that flew over places like Berlin and Tokyo. Nobody talked about it, and posters were everywhere in Monument, pasted to the sides of buildings: A SLIP OF THE LIP MAY SINK A SHIP. "My father drinks too much but he never misses a day of work," Kathleen Mary said.

"Was Dad like Mr. O'Hara when he drank?" I asked my mother.

"All drinkers are different," she said. "Your father got dreamy. He'd get a silly grin on his face and sit in his chair and sometimes he'd try to sing some old song. Then he'd fall asleep. The bad times were when he wouldn't come home at night. He'd roam the streets for hours. Sometimes the cops brought him home. They never locked him up, because he was always a gentleman, even when he was drunk. Then the next day he'd be filled with guilt and was too ashamed to look at me. He'd promise not to drink again, ever, and would go weeks sometimes without the drink and then he'd start again. He never kept his promises until you were born, Darcy. But he was always gentle, drunk or sober."

❖❖❖

"Living in Frenchtown is like living in an opera," my father had said when we first arrived and we heard the people talking in the stores or calling to each other from porch to porch, their voices like a special kind of music.

They spoke very quickly, their words blending together and their hands flying everywhere as if they were speaking in sign language at the same time.

When Mrs. LeBlanc downstairs called to neighbors passing on the sidewalk and they chatted awhile, my father waved his arms like a music conductor, his baton invisible, directing the unseen music from our porch. In the stores on Third Street, the rapid-fire exchanges between clerks and customers were a marvel to my ears. Not only was it like living in an opera, it was also like living in a foreign country.

Mr. and Mrs. LeBlanc, downstairs on the first floor, spent most of their time that summer on the porch, speaking to people as they passed. Mr. LeBlanc was bald and wore suspenders. He was a boss at one of the factories, my mother said, and spoke English quite well, always commenting on the weather when we passed. He and his wife had no children. "It's hard to believe they're Canucks," Kathleen Mary said. "No children, and Mr. LeBlanc doesn't butcher the English language."

Above us, on the third floor, lived two old ladies,

the Lombard sisters, who seldom ventured from their tenement, even to sit on the porch. They went to church every Sunday wearing coats and dresses so long they almost covered their shoes, holding each other's arms, looking neither right nor left. Their hats were identical, straw picture hats with a black ribbon around the brim. We often heard them walking across the floor above us, their footsteps heavy and slow as if they never took off their shoes, even late in the evening or when one of them got up in the middle of the night. Otherwise the tenement upstairs might as well have been vacant.

"You're lucky for the peace and quiet," Kathleen Mary said. "We got thirty people—I counted them—living in our three-decker, and the only peace we get is Sunday when everybody goes to church. And I'm not even there to enjoy it."

Sunday was church day for Kathleen Mary. She was always gorgeously arrayed in a dress—most likely some shade of yellow, her favorite color—with shining black patent-leather shoes and socks to match her dress. I envied her as she walked past my house and waved to me. My envy had nothing to do with religion but with belonging. Belonging to a church, a parish, a something. My father and mother had not joined a church after our arrival in Monument. I reported to my mother one day that a Unitarian Church was located next to the Monument Public Library. The church featured a framed bulletin board on its front lawn with quotations printed in letters big enough to see from across the street. Quotations like TO ERR IS HUMAN, TO FORGIVE DIVINE, or TO THINE OWN SELF BE TRUE.

"We'll go to church when we can go as a family," my mother said. I knew what that meant: when the war was over.

Sundays were the longest and loneliest days of the week, as far as I was concerned. Sometimes I did not see Kathleen Mary at all. After attending church in the morning, which she called celebrating the mass, she returned in the afternoon for something called catechism. In the evening there was often a meeting of the Children of Mary.

"The children of who?" I asked, the first time she mentioned that meeting. I was a bit angry because these children were taking Kathleen Mary away from me on Sunday evenings.

"Mary," she said. "The Holy Virgin Mary, Mother of God."

"Oh," was all I could manage, faintly ashamed at disparaging such an impressive figure.

"It's an organization," Kathleen Mary explained,

going into one of her speeches. "Its real name is the Sodality of the Children of Mary. You have to be a girl to belong. No boys allowed."

"But what do you *do*?" I asked, still a bit piqued.

"We do good works," she said, sounding like she was quoting a great authority. "We pray. We help the war effort by making bandages. Some of us are picked to place a crown of flowers on the heads of brides during their wedding."

The Sodality of the Children of Mary intrigued me. But then everything about Kathleen Mary's Catholicism fascinated me, as if Catholics were a different tribe of people who had somehow found their way to earth. Kathleen Mary delighted in explaining the strange practices of Catholics, which gave her an opportunity to make more speeches.

Like not eating meat on Friday.

Going to confession every Saturday afternoon.

Receiving communion on the first Friday of every month.

Praying for the souls in purgatory.

Purgatory?

Purgatory was a terrible waiting room between heaven and hell where you might get stuck forever unless your family offered prayers and arranged for masses at the church.

How do you arrange for masses?

You buy them, from the priest, at the rectory. A dollar for a low mass, two dollars for a high mass.

Buy masses? Like bribes to God?

Right, Kathleen Mary said. God likes being bribed if the bribe is a good thing.

And communion. Receiving the white wafer—not really a wafer but somehow God himself—into your mouth, on your tongue, careful not to let the wafer touch your teeth.

I listened, wide-eyed, in awe and wonder, as she told me of mortal sin and venial sin.

Categories of sin?

Yes, even worse: cardinal sins. Really big ones.

"How about you, Darcy? How about your religion? You never go to church."

"I'm a Unitarian," I said.

"What's a Unitarian?"

Because I wasn't certain, I said, "Like a Catholic, only not so strict. We don't have confession or communion. Or purgatory. And my father says that the pope is an old man in Rome who should mind his own *P*'s and *Q*'s."

"Do you have sin?" Kathleen Mary asked. I looked at her sharply to see whether she was serious or joking about Unitarians.

"I guess so," I said. "I mean, if sin is doing something bad, then we have it. But we don't have to confess or anything."

"What do you do, then? I mean, how do you get rid of your sins? How do you clean your soul of the stain of sin?"

"I don't know," I said, shocked by the knowledge that I was walking around with my soul stained with sin.

My mother did her best to explain it all to me when I went home, reeling with Kathleen Mary's information.

Carefully ironing my blue dress, the one with the lace collar, she said, "Of course your soul is not stained with sin, Darcy. You're a good girl. Your soul is pure."

"But what *if* my soul gets stained, how do I get it cleaned up if I can't go to confession like Kathleen Mary?"

"Unitarians like us don't go to confession, but that doesn't mean God does not forgive us," she said, hanging the dress up, then leaning on the ironing board. "Kathleen Mary confesses to a priest because that's a rule for Catholics. But without God there would be no forgiving. All you have to do, Darcy, is ask God to forgive you. He will, if you are sincere."

"Then I don't need a priest?" I said, immeasurably relieved.

"Of course not."

"Priests are only go-betweens," I said, pleased

with my sudden grasp of the process. "Between God and people."

"Something like that," my mother said. "You don't need a priest to go to heaven."

"Listen, I'm sick of all this crap," Kathleen Mary announced one hot June day when even the dandelions drooped on the small patches of lawn in front of the tenements.

"What crap?" I asked, delighted to be using a word from Kathleen Mary's vocabulary.

"This childhood crap. I want to grow up. I want to have the Curse. I want coconuts."

"Coconuts?"

"You know, these things," she said, pointing to her chest.

Coconuts I could understand, although I didn't particularly want them. But I wondered about that other thing she mentioned.

"What's the Curse?" I asked, automatically elevating the word to a capital letter simply from the tone of her voice.

"The monthlies. The period. What makes us women, when it finally comes." Then despairing: "If it ever comes."

I nodded, remembering my mother's feeble explanation about what happens to girls sooner or later as they grow up. She was so ill at ease in providing the information, however, that I had asked no unnecessary questions, content to wait for puberty, which sounded like a better word than the Curse, to show up.

"Know what we've got to do?" Kathleen Mary asked. Those words were always a call to adventure, especially on that sultry Saturday in our first week of summer vacation.

"If you've got the plan, I've got the time," I said, a variation of my father's favorite answer.

"We will take our own first steps toward becoming women."

"How do we do that?" I asked.

"We do away with childish things, like it says in the Bible." Seeing my frown, she said, "You still have Shirley Temple, don't you? And your paper dolls?"

I nodded, not speaking, dreading whatever plan she had devised.

"And I still have my Jane Withers hat," she said.

"So what do we do with them?" I asked, squinting in the sunlight, not really wanting to hear the answer to my question.

"We could burn them," Kathleen Mary suggested. "That would be highly symbolic. Or we could give them to the war effort—you know, *Slap the Japs with Scrap*—but I don't think Shirley Temple doll stuff and a Jane Withers hat would win any battles."

I wanted to say, "Maybe we should simply keep them," thinking of Shirley guarding me through all the nights on the bureau and all the conversations we'd had, all the troubles of my life she had listened to.

"I know," Kathleen Mary announced in sudden decision, leaping to her feet. "The Salvation Army. They give to poor people. We can take our stuff there and leave it for them to give to the truly deserving."

Who are the truly deserving? I wondered, looking at the three-deckers, the old and faded clothing hanging on clotheslines, the dusty streets, the pathetic backyard gardens, the absence of any softness in Frenchtown.

"Nobody is poor here in Frenchtown anymore," Kathleen Mary said. "Everybody's either working in the shops or gone off to fight. But somewhere there must be children without dolls or hats, and the Salvation Army will find them."

I assented reluctantly, finding Kathleen Mary impossible to resist when she began making a speech. "Besides," she said, "this idea may be an omen. Maybe it will bring on the Curse."

That possibility almost made me change my mind.

Later that day we trudged up Mechanic Street and across Monument Square to the Salvation Army headquarters.

Later that day we trudged up Mechanic Street and across Monument Square to the Salvation Army headquarters in a store next to the five-and-ten. Shirley Temple and the paper dolls were in a cardboard box I had found in the shed. Kathleen Mary had meticulously wrapped her Jane Withers hat in tissue paper.

A tall, thin woman with black-rimmed glasses perched on her nose smiled at us as we entered with our packages. A ribbon dangled from her glasses. The glasses had no stems. I was awed by those glasses and vowed someday to own a pair, although they would not be practical for running or climbing over fences.

"What a lovely, generous thing to do," she said, accepting our donations. "You'll make some children very very happy."

I could not help staring at her glasses.

That night, her glasses forgotten, I wept inconsolably in my bed, muffling my sobs so that my mother would not hear them. I realized that I did not want to be a woman, and certainly did not want the Curse as I mourned the passing of Shirley Temple from my life.

"*W*e're going to church tomorrow," my mother said, as she handed me a copy of the *Monument Times,* a page of which she had neatly folded.

Two or three columns of church listings were printed on the page, and my eyes quickly found a schedule with *Unitarian Church* appearing at the top. *"The Rev. Wilmot Deems, pastor. Sunday Service at 10 a.m. Prelude, Hymn, Sermon by the Reverend Mr. Deems, Postlude . . .*

"I think your father would approve," she said.

I was elated. For at least part of one Sunday I would not face the empty hours alone. The service would also provide an opportunity to pray for my father in a setting that should transmit my prayers directly to God without any outside intervention. A silly thought, I knew, but I somehow gained comfort from it.

As my mother and I walked up Mechanic Street toward the center of town the next day, I reveled in the feeling of Sunday morning. Streets quiet, no shouts of children playing. The people we met were dressed up in their best clothes and smiled politely as we greeted each other. Most of them were French Canadians on their way to St. Jude's, while my mother and I were the only people headed toward downtown.

"I always loved going to church with you and Daddy," I said, holding her hand. Which wasn't exactly true. What I liked was the three of us going somewhere as a family, because, to be honest, church services often bored me, consisting as they often did of wheezy organ playing that made my father wince. He'd often make faces at me, causing me to stifle my laughter and my mother to bristle. The sermons were unending as the minister preached about subjects that had no meaning in my life. The favorite word of the minister, Reverend Goss in Clapham, was *perdition.* He scattered the word like confetti throughout his talk, and I did not know what it meant exactly although I could guess at its meaning given the context. However, I never bothered to look it up in the dictionary.

"You're a good girl, Darcy," my mother said. "You've been very patient with us, traveling the country, never settling down."

I knew this did not require an answer and placed my arm around her waist and pressed against her.

Reverend Wilmot Deems turned out to be an old man, thin and trembling, who slowly and excruciatingly struggled across the sanctuary. He waited a few moments to catch his breath before mounting the pulpit; his wheezing and gasping echoed throughout the church. Something in his throat rattled, and he spent a bit more time trying to clear it with coughs and sputterings. The congregation was patient, waiting, no one moving, all focused on the old man as he prepared to speak.

Despite his age and his throat trouble, Reverend Wilmot Deems spoke forcefully from the pulpit as if he had reserved all of his strength for this sermon. His hands did not tremble as they clutched the wooden pulpit. He used simple words as if he were addressing small children, and it felt good to be treated like children, as if we were in good hands, safe and secure.

"Be like the lilies of the field, who do not toil or spin. Be like flowers everywhere, who respond to rain and sunshine and need nothing else. Be like trees that stretch to the sky."

His words were like music, and I thought of my father and his love of music. The minister's words were also gentle strokings, and I found myself almost floating away, drowsy, contented, thinking of myself as a flower in a field of green, peaceful and serene as the sun shone upon me.

A burst of organ chords and voices singing "Praise the Lord and Pass the Ammunition" startled me from my reverie, and I looked up at my mother, who was singing rousingly along with the rest of the congregation. Leaping to my feet, I joined them, my voice blending with the other voices. My mother placed her hand on my shoulder. I could have stood there singing forever.

———❖❖❖———

"The bells of St. Jude don't ring anymore," Kathleen Mary said one day as we walked by the church. "They used to ring three times a day. The Angelus. Morning, noon, and suppertime." Then, with her usual air of authority: "They won't ring again until the war is over."

"I'd love to hear them," I said, thinking how the

sound of bells would soften the starkness of Frenchtown. There were more telephone poles than trees along Frenchtown streets.

"Not everybody loved the bells," she said. "They woke up babies and old people from their naps. Rang at six o'clock in the morning, for crying out loud, and got all of Frenchtown out of bed."

"I'd still love to hear them," I persisted.

Never one to be deterred, she said, "Don't worry, Darcy. We'll find other bells to ring."

I believed her, although I could not imagine what those other bells would be.

We paused to look up at the highest steeple, and I imagined the sound of bells coming from it, growing dizzy as I gazed into the sky beyond the steeple, but a pleasant dizziness. Tearing my eyes away, I looked around for Kathleen Mary. She had disappeared.

"Kathleen Mary, where are you?" I called. I ran to the corner. She was not there. I called her name again.

"Surprise," she said, stepping from an alcove near the door.

"Stop being childish," I scolded. "I thought you had deserted me."

"I would never desert you, Darcy," she said. Was she serious or joking? "That's a promise."

Kathleen Mary did disappear from my life on occasion. She would not call my name from the sidewalk below, did not summon me to adventures I could not resist. One afternoon when I had not heard from her for a day or two, I walked the seven blocks to her house. She was not at home. Her mother was uncommunicative as usual, waving her hand vaguely when I asked where Kathleen Mary was, as if the effort to speak was too much for her to bear. Her brothers—John Francis, Joseph Patrick, and Billy Vincent—were equally silent, ignoring me almost completely, acting as if I did not exist on the planet Earth, although they were willing taunters when I met them on the street with the other boys in their gang.

"Where do you think she could be?" I asked, for the third or fourth time.

They lounged on the porch in silent conspiracy, unusually quiet and morose, which made me look at them closer, something I usually avoided doing. I saw things I had not noticed at first. A bruise on Joseph Patrick's cheek, Billy Vincent's black eye, which was not really black but purple. John Francis seemed to have escaped injury, but I noticed that he held himself awkwardly as he leaned against the banister. None of their eyes met mine.

"Was your father on a rampage again?" I asked, shocked at my boldness.

"Mind your own business," John Francis
muttered.

I knew then that it was time to leave, and
I retreated, taking one of Kathleen Mary's shortcuts through the backyards of Mechanic Street.
As I pondered whether to climb a fence or take the
long way around the Chouinard property, a voice
called my name. I turned to find John Francis
standing a few feet away. His eyes were large and
mournful in his thin face, and his arms were wrapped
around his chest as if to keep his ribs from coming
apart.

"Are you injured?" I asked.

"Injured," he scoffed. "Do you always have to
talk fancy?"

I did not realize I had been talking fancy. "Are
you hurt?" I asked.

He shrugged, and the effort caused a flash in his
eyes, like pain becoming visible. "Listen, Darcy. I'm
sorry for telling you to mind your own business. But
he's our father. And he only hits us when he's
drinking."

But he's drinking most of the time, I wanted to
say. Instead, I asked, "Did he hit Kathleen Mary?"

"No, and he better not," John Francis said. "Or
I'll kill him."

"Where is she, anyway?"

Again the shrug. Again the wince of pain. "Hiding out someplace, I guess."

"Did he hurt you bad, John Francis?"

"Naw, I got in his way and he threw me against the wall, but I didn't bleed or anything."

John Francis was fifteen, but he had the face of an old man, wizened cheeks, his hair a dull orange, squinting blue eyes that the sun seemed to hurt. He was Kathleen Mary's favorite brother. "He's my protector," she told me once, and I had wondered, Protector against what? Now I knew.

That evening Kathleen Mary showed up at my house, not calling my name but sitting on the steps until I wandered out to the porch and discovered her when I glanced over the banister.

"Where have you been, Kathleen Mary?" I said.

"Hiding out," she explained. "John Francis said you came looking for me. Poor John Francis. My father was chasing me and my mother through the rooms, and John Francis stopped him."

"Why didn't you call the cops or something?"

"It's nobody's business but ours," Kathleen Mary said, hands on hips, ready for an argument. "But he's getting worse. I wish he didn't have that bad leg, so that he'd get drafted and go to war or something," she said. "Kill some Japs before he kills one of us."

Twenty-four hours later my father stood in our

45

kitchen and announced that he was being sent overseas.

Where the fighting was going on.

"No details," my father said, resplendent in his dress uniform, brass buttons shining and his eyes shining too. But his mouth fragile, quivering a bit when he talked. "I'm not even supposed to be here, but my sergeant gave me a quick pass."

A jeep stood outside, motor running, exhaust curling from its tailpipe, a soldier behind the wheel smoking a cigarette while neighborhood kids gathered around inspecting the vehicle.

"Only time for a kiss and a couple of hugs," my father said, beckoning to us.

He sank down on the couch as my mother and I surrounded him, my mother murmuring soft things against his chest. I felt odd, as if I was there in his arms and yet somewhere in an audience, as if we were acting out a scene in a movie at the Plymouth where the hero goes off to war and music plays in the background. But we were not in a movie. Tears began to blur my vision, and I tried to blink them away. My father was going to a place where men died.

"Cheer up, Darcy," he said, thumbing away a tear on my cheek. "The sooner I go, the sooner I'll be back. I'm not the only one, you know. Thousands of guys like me are going too. Have gone already."

"But you seem so happy about it," I said.

I was aware of my mother sitting in silence.

"I'm both happy and unhappy at the same time," he said. "I want to go and I want to stay. But going is the right thing to do." He glanced at my mother, and so did I, and she smiled but her smile looked like it was pasted on.

My father's eyes were bright and snapping, all the wistfulness gone, although his lips trembled a bit, like a small boy the moment before he bursts out crying.

"I'll be fine," he said, looking at my mother again. "I'll take it one day at a time." *One day at a time*—his secret AA message to my mother. She had told me about the AA slogans, like "one day at a time" and "easy does it."

"We'll be fine too," she told him, drawing me to her. And my father stretched his arms out to embrace us both.

We sat like that until the jeep's horn sounded, and a minute later he was gone.

———❖❖❖———

47

My mother went to work at Viscoid, where she inspected sheets of Lucite for flaws, small bubbles, or tiny, almost-invisible blemishes that she had to squint to see. "Lucite comes out of the machines warm and must be kept clear," she said. "Even tiny pieces of lint in the air can spoil a sheet." Women working in factories were required to have short hair or tuck their long hair into a snood or bandanna to eliminate the danger of getting their hair caught in a machine. My mother cut her hair, which emphasized her cheekbones and made her eyes seem bigger. Dark smudges were like black crayon marks under her eyes. Her headaches increased, and she spent hours in the darkened bedroom with a wet towel over her eyes. "We can use the money, Darcy, and I'm also contributing to the war effort," she said.

My contributions were meager—collecting whatever scrap metal Kathleen Mary and I found scrounging the neighborhood and back alleys of Third Street, like old tin cans that we flattened or old newspapers that we turned in at collection centers. We were not very successful. Everyone else was looking for stuff like that, and the streets of America, or at least Frenchtown, had probably never been so clear of litter and debris.

My mother was fortunate not to be assigned to the night shift, from 3:00 P.M. to 11:00 P.M., or the graveyard shift, which ran through the night until seven o'clock in the morning. She worked daytimes from seven in the morning until three in the afternoon, but her days off were rotated, so that she often was away from the tenement on Saturdays and Sundays and I was left at loose ends on those days.

One warm Saturday afternoon as Frenchtown drowsed in the August sunshine, Kathleen Mary greeted me with an expression on her face that I instantly recognized: She had a plan!

"Let's go," she said.

I followed languorously, looking forward to whatever adventure she had in mind, but caught in the lassitude of the sleepy day. On the porches people sat in the shadows, away from the sunlight.

"Come on," Kathleen Mary called impatiently, waiting for me to catch up.

We passed by the stores on Third Street, and Kathleen Mary refused to window-shop, one of our favorite recreations. She led me through a series of shortcuts that took us to the three buildings that formed the center of Frenchtown: St. Jude's Church, the parochial school next door, and the convent, which stood beside the school.

She paused in front of the convent, studying the tall, forbidding structure as I approached. Although its shutters did not sag and the windows were clean and sparkling, the four-story building reminded me of haunted houses in the movies. Surrounded by a maze of high hedges, the convent seemed to be hugging secrets to itself.

"Follow me," Kathleen Mary said, walking confidently up the front walk, her head held high as usual.

At a spot halfway to the front door she slipped into an opening in the hedges and motioned for me to follow.

"You could get lost in here," she said, noting how the hedges, at least six feet tall, were laid out in crisscross fashion. "But I know how to get around."

We made our way around corners and through narrow passageways. Kathleen Mary kept up a running commentary in her best confidential voice.

"The nuns sleep up there on the fourth floor," she said, pointing to the top of the building. "Those windows are never open. They sleep in their heavy underwear, winter or summer."

I did not question where Kathleen Mary had obtained her information.

As we went forward, turned corners, and seemed to be making no progress toward our mysterious destination, she said, "Nuns are paid ten cents a week."

Shocked, I said, "That's terrible."

"They don't mind, because they're brides of Christ. That keeps them happy. Christ is their bridegroom."

I found this impossible to believe and did not dignify it with a response.

"No fooling, Darcy. Every nun wears a wedding ring. Look for it when you see one of them. Every nun is married to Christ. When she takes her vows, it's like a wedding."

Ten cents a week, brides of Christ. I shook my head as we ducked around a corner and approached a latticed fence that enclosed a small courtyard. She stopped abruptly, and I bumped into her. My body was damp with perspiration, and the afternoon heat seemed concentrated on us in the hedges. Turning to me, Kathleen Mary placed a long finger against her lips. I had no intention of speaking anyway. The latticed fence provided privacy for the courtyard but allowed us to peek through the slats. We were also protected from detection by the thick, overgrown shrubbery.

Emulating Kathleen Mary, I peered through the bushes to see what was going on in the courtyard. Actually not much was going on. A tiny nun sat on a marble bench under a trellised archway where pink roses bloomed. She was so small her feet barely touched the cement floor of the courtyard. I could not see her face because it was enclosed by a kind of black shawl that covered her head, hiding her hair. Two nuns stood on either side of her, like guardians, in their black-and-white costumes. Habits, Kathleen

51

"That's Sister Angela," she whispered, indicating the tiny nun. "Some people say she's a saint."

Mary called the costumes. Other nuns stood nearby like sentinels.

"That's Sister Angela," she whispered, indicating the tiny nun. "Some people say she's a saint. People come to her from miles around for cures."

At that moment a tall blond woman appeared carrying a child in her arms. The child's legs were in steel braces. Her long black hair, like mine, fell to her shoulders. Arriving in front of the nun, the woman put the child down. The child stood awkwardly in the courtyard, the sunlight glinting on the braces.

Sister Angela held out her arms, and the child struggled toward her, flinging herself finally at the nun. After embracing her for a moment Sister Angela made room for the child on the bench. As the nun turned, I saw her eyes. Clear blue eyes, as if she had only looked at beautiful things. She gestured above the child's head.

"The sign of the cross," Kathleen Mary hissed softly.

"I know that," I said.

Sister Angela made small crosses with her thumb on the child's forehead and cheeks and chin. She embraced the little girl, murmuring words I could not catch.

"She's praying, in Latin," Kathleen Mary explained.

I waited breathlessly as the child stood up, expecting her to throw off her braces and walk triumphantly away, crippled no longer. Instead she rose laboriously, by degrees, until she stood on her feet, breathing deeply from the effort. She smiled wanly at Sister Angela and reached up to take her mother's hand. Her mother picked her up and carried her away.

"She didn't get cured," I said to Kathleen Mary, disappointed.

"It doesn't happen like that," Kathleen Mary whispered, snapping her fingers, the sound magnified in the silence of the afternoon. "It might happen tomorrow or next week. Miracles take time."

The cynical side of me, perhaps my father's Unitarian side, said, "Or maybe never."

Kathleen accepted my skepticism with a shrug of her shoulders. "Sometimes miracles are not physical," she said. "Maybe that kid still won't be able to walk, but she'll *feel* better. See? There's all kinds of cures." She returned to her vigil, and so did I.

This time a young woman slowly approached Sister Angela. Beautiful in a white lace dress, a lace handkerchief plopped on the top of her head. "She looks like a movie star," I whispered.

As she drew closer, I saw her eyes. Big eyes, dark eyes, haunted eyes, as if they had looked upon horrors no mortal should ever see. She approached Sister Angela as if in a trance and knelt at her feet.

Sister Angela took the young woman's face into her hands, enclosing her face with her fingers. She leaned forward until their faces almost touched, as if the nun were trying to look past her eyes, deep into her brain, into her soul maybe. The young woman closed her eyes finally, and her shoulders drooped, as if she had fallen asleep there on her knees. The nun spoke softly, words I could not hear, prayers no doubt. They remained there awhile, the nun praying, the young woman with her eyes closed. Silence and stillness pervaded the courtyard. I was not aware of Kathleen Mary's presence, or of the heat of the afternoon or the smell of the hedges, caught up as I was in that tableau of tenderness in the courtyard. Finally the young woman opened her eyes. The other nuns stirred as if emerging from sleep. And I, too, suddenly seemed to come awake, alive to the sounds of birds singing, a dog barking somewhere in the distance.

I watched the young woman walk away from the nun. Was her step lighter? Was there a smile on her face? Her eyes no longer haunted? I could not see her face, could not tell what had happened, and had no answers to those questions as she disappeared from view.

For the next hour or so a sad procession passed

before the old nun. People on crutches or leaning on canes for support. Limping, hobbling, in braces and bandages, struggling to place one foot before another. Young and old. Men, women, and children. Dull eyes suddenly flashing with pain. I thought of all the misery in the world—could Sister Angela cure them all? Or any of them? Those who sought her help hobbled away, still on crutches, with their canes, stumbling sometimes, the way they had come, unchanged by the visit. Miracles take time, Kathleen Mary had said. If they happened at all, that is.

When the last of the visitors had departed, Sister Angela sighed and closed her eyes, her shoulders slumping in weariness. Immediately one of the guardian nuns bent over her and dabbed her forehead with a handkerchief. She turned toward the others and clapped her hands twice. A bell rang distantly somewhere inside the convent. Two nuns came forward and assisted the old nun to her feet. She walked slowly across the courtyard, her feet invisible under the long black skirt, almost as if she were floating an inch or two above the floor. A moment later the courtyard was deserted.

"All done for today," Kathleen Mary said.

"Does this happen every day?" I asked.

"Only on weekends," she said. "Sister Angela is famous. People come from miles around. It's a big secret and yet it's not a secret. I mean, nobody talks about it much. I heard that a newspaper reporter came to the convent once to do a story but they wouldn't let him in. I don't think men are allowed in there, anyway."

"Does she really cure people?" I asked, thinking of the child who limped and the young woman with the haunted eyes.

"Would they come if she didn't?" she asked, her voice snapping with the old sassiness of Kathleen Mary O'Hara.

———❖❖❖———

Now that my father was overseas, our daily mail became important. Each day I waited for the mailman and watched his slow progress toward our house in his gray suit and visored hat, sighing as he shifted the mail bag from one shoulder to the other or stopped to chat with people along the way. Wisps of gray hair escaped from his cap, and his white mustache drooped at the corners of his mouth. I grew impatient waiting for him. When he reached our house and riffled through the letters in his worn leather bag, I hoped to see the blue-gray envelope with the red border that meant, of course, a letter from my father.

Until my father shipped out to Europe, our war

had been confined to the streets of Frenchtown and consisted of ration stamps and food shortages—*No Butter Today, No Ifs, Ands, Or Butts*—and factory chimneys belching smoke twenty-four hours a day. At the Plymouth Theater, the newsreels—*The Eyes and Ears of the World*—brought the war close to us with bombs and tanks and burned-out cities and men fighting and falling. Strange names flashed on the screen—Saipan and Tobruk and Guadalcanal. Now, still another war, the war of loneliness and heartache and waiting, came to us in letters bearing an APO postmark on paper as thin as peeling sunburn.

My father's letters were infrequent and brief, his words guarded because his location and activities had to be kept secret from an enemy who might intercept the mail. Although his letters included no real news, they served to let us know that he was alive. Every day was filled with both expectancy and dread, and my mother's first words on arriving home from the factory were "Any letter today?"

Saturday morning in Frenchtown. An August morning with heat already sizzling in the air and people on their porches fanning themselves with folded newspapers or the butterfly-shaped fans obtained at Laurier's Drugstore with any purchase of twenty-five cents or more. My mother was at the Lucite plant, and I had completed the chores she had assigned: changing the sheets of our beds, wet-mopping the kitchen floor, and washing and drying the breakfast dishes.

Kathleen Mary O'Hara waited for me at the bottom of the stoop. All dolled up in a pink, lacy dress and white patent-leather shoes. On a Saturday morning?

"Want to be a Girl Scout?" she asked, her hectic hair in vivid contrast to the paleness of pink.

"We're not old enough," I said warily, wondering what new scheme or exploit she was about to unveil. "You have to be twelve to be a Scout."

"I know that," she said. "But there's a meeting of the Children of Mary today, and a Girl Scout official is going to speak about scouting and how we can join as soon as we turn twelve."

Our birthdays were less than a week apart, mine on November 19th and Kathleen Mary's three days later.

"I'm not one of the Children of Mary," I said. Admiring her dress and envying the way Kathleen Mary was always at ease with the world, whether in dress, overalls, or hand-me-down pants, I added, "And I'm not dressed up."

"You're always dressed up," she said. Which in a way was true. That day my mother had left me a plaid cotton skirt and white blouse to wear with black patent-leather shoes. "And you don't have to be a Child of Mary for this meeting. You'll be my guest."

"Where is this meeting?" I asked, still tentative, not wanting to venture where I did not belong.

"In the church basement at St. Brendan's."

"I've never been in a Catholic church before," I said. "Don't you have to wear a hat?"

"We're not going *into* the church, Darcy. We'll walk through the vestibule and go down the steps to the basement. I don't have a hat on, do I?"

Reluctantly I assented and followed, slightly behind, as usual, as Kathleen Mary walked briskly up Mechanic Street. A few minutes later as we approached St. Brendan's, my footsteps faltered. The red-brick building with its twin massive steeples high above the front entrance loomed over us forbiddingly.

"I can't go in there," I said.

Kathleen Mary sighed in exasperation.

"Why not?"

"Because I'm Protestant. A Unitarian."

"Who's going to know?" she asked, rolling her eyes. "You don't look like a Unitarian."

I shook my head at this absurdity, not sure whether Kathleen Mary was joking with me.

"Come on," she said, cutting across the lawn in front of the rectory, where the priests lived. Kathleen Mary always took shortcuts, across lawns, into alleys, through the side exits at the Plymouth.

More reluctant than ever, I did not follow her passage over the lawn but went the long way around, on the sidewalk and then slowly up the cement walkway leading to the front steps of the church, where Kathleen Mary waited, tapping her foot.

"Darcy, look upon this as a grand adventure," she said. "They say that you can make a wish when you visit a church you've never been in before."

"I don't believe in wishes," I said.

"Don't you blow out the candles on your birthday cake and make a wish?" She led me up the stone stairs as she talked, then pulled open the huge door that swung slowly on creaking hinges.

We stepped into the vestibule, dim and cool, our footsteps echoing on the marble floor. The stained-glass doors to the church proper were closed, for which I was grateful, making me feel less an interloper entering forbidden territory.

Kathleen Mary beckoned me to a marble pedestal standing next to the church door. A large basin of water stood on the pedestal.

"Holy water," Kathleen Mary said, dipping her hand in the bowl and touching her forehead, shoulders, and chest with her wet fingers, making the sign of the cross.

A spot of moisture remained on her forehead, glistening in the subdued light.

She dipped her fingers in the bowl once more.

Then turned to me.

She sprinkled me with the holy water. Drops of

water struck my cheeks, splashed into my eye, made me blink. A drop ran down my cheek, like a misplaced tear.

"Now you're a Catholic, Darcy Webster," she said. "Forever and ever, world without end, Amen."

Stunned, I said, "What?"

"I said you're a Catholic. A Roman Catholic. I sprinkled you with holy water. Roman Catholic holy water."

I studied her face, searching for a glimpse of the imp in Kathleen Mary that would tell me she was only joking. But she regarded me curiously, as if she expected an instant change in my personality.

At that moment a group of chattering, laughing girls invaded the vestibule, obviously on their way to the Children of Mary meeting. Kathleen Mary called out to them, "Wait for us." A lot of commotion for a church vestibule. "Come on, Darcy," she urged as she joined the newcomers.

"I'm not coming," I said, but she didn't hear me as she chatted with the girls, all the while walking toward a doorway at the right side of the entrance. She seemed to have forgotten my presence. Finally, at the doorway, she turned and motioned for me to come with her. I hung back, shaking my head as she disappeared from sight, carried along by the other girls.

I made my escape from the church, down the stone steps, out into the August heat and the glare of the sun. I was eager to go home, to look at myself in a mirror to see if I had somehow changed. Don't be ridiculous, I told myself, this is just another of Kathleen Mary's antics. But I hurried along anyway, ignoring the heat, wiping the steam from my glasses with my handkerchief. A bit of holy water can't make you a Catholic, can it? Can it? I did not know the answer, did not know the rules of the Catholic Church. I knew vaguely that water and baptism went together, that some people were dipped into water when they were baptized. Didn't John the Baptist baptize Jesus Christ in the River Jordan? My thoughts were all jumbled as I walked down Mechanic Street, faster and faster, as if I were being chased all the way home.

———◆◆◆———

Kathleen Mary began one of her absences.

I did not see her the rest of that day. Or the next. Which I understood, because that next day was Sunday and she would be busy at St. Brendan's: morning mass, afternoon catechism, and the Children of Mary in the evening.

A small part of me was relieved by her absence. I was not sure how I felt about her. Had she sprinkled me with holy water as a joke? I realized again how difficult it always was for me to tell whether she was joking or serious, sarcastic or sincere.

Actually I did not feel Catholic.

Had no urge to go to church. Or to receive communion.

A heavy burden was lifted from me because of the lack of Catholic symptoms.

But I was also impatient for Kathleen Mary to show up and put all my doubts to rest.

———✥✥✥———

Somewhere in Europe, Aug. 18
Dear Darcy:
I am writing this late at night. I have been thinking of you because today we marched through ——— and little kids waved to us as we went by. One of them was a girl about your age. At that moment I realized how much I miss you.

I'm fine. The work of engineers is interesting. And important. Without our bridges, our soldiers would not be able to

*advance. Don't worry about me, though. We
build bridges before the battles begin and we
repair them after the battles end.*

*Take good care of your mother, Darcy.
Kiss her for me and give her a big hug. Tell
her I am taking it one day at a time.*
*Every night when I go to sleep, I think of you
both. I can't wait to come home.*

*With loads of love and barrels of kisses,
Your Dad*

That blank space in the middle of a sentence was
terrifying. The army censor had omitted the name of
the town my father had marched through, which
made it seem as if he was no place on earth. I could
not point to a map and say, "My father is there."

Yet his letter cheered me up. When I read it
aloud, his words came to life as if he were actually
talking to me. I went to sleep that night with that
sentence singing in my mind: *I can't wait to come
home.*

But the next morning I thought immediately of
Kathleen Mary and wondered, Do I feel Catholic?
How is a Catholic supposed to feel?

I could swear that my flesh still felt moist and

tingled where the drop of holy water had traced a path down my cheek.

I touched my cheek tentatively and was surprised to find that my fingers came away dry.

As I left the bed, yawning, I vowed that I would track Kathleen Mary down today and find out once and for all whether she had made me a Catholic.

Kathleen Mary's three-decker seemed to be dozing in the afternoon stillness, and her name floated forlornly on the air as I called to her. Something disturbed me as I called her name again, scrutinizing her house. Something else beside the stillness. What was wrong? I called her name a third time.

Still no answer.

There were no curtains in the windows of her tenement. That's what was wrong. As I made that discovery, old Mrs. Lamoureux emerged from her tenement and tottered toward the porch banister.

Looking down at me, she said, "All gone, move away." Her French accent was so thick I had to grope for its meaning. Which came soon enough.

"Big fight," Mrs. Lamoureux said, shaking her head dolefully. "Police come, take O'Hara away.

There were no curtains in the windows of her tenement.
That's what was wrong.

O'Hara beat up everybodies." Then, turning her mouth down in contempt: "Irishers."

"When did this happen?" I asked, searching the windows and porch for clues I knew did not exist.

"Days two," she said, holding up two fingers. "Truck he come, boys pile furniture on, all go away."

But Kathleen Mary was my best friend, I wanted to shout, in protest and disbelief. She would not leave me like that, without a final message of farewell. She had promised that she would never desert me. Hope flashed within me as I thought that she might have left a note with my mother who had forgotten to give it to me. Or maybe she had slipped it into our mailbox.

As Mrs. Lamoureux shuffled back to her doorway, still shaking her head no doubt at the antics of Irishers, I sped homeward, holding on to my glasses, glad for the pigtails that kept my hair away from my face so that I could run faster. I arrived home out of breath, heart beating furiously as I bounded up the stairs.

My mother was already home from work, sitting in the chair near the radio, but I was instantly dismayed when I saw the moist facecloth of her forehead and her eyes shattered and raw-looking.

"Another headache?" I asked. Her headaches often sent her to bed and isolated her from me. And I needed her desperately at this moment, needed to discuss Kathleen Mary's departure with her. Who else was there to talk to?

"My eyes, Darcy," my mother murmured. "Inspecting that Lucite is like looking at the sun all day."

Later, after taking a bath and swallowing some aspirin, she called me into the bedroom, where she lay on the counterpane, eyes closed, cheeks taut with pain.

"What's the matter, Darcy?" She could always detect my unhappiness.

I told her about Kathleen Mary's departure, her entire family gone from Frenchtown without a word of warning.

"Poor Darcy," she crooned softly, reaching out to me, gathering me into her arms. "Maybe it's only temporary. Maybe she'll come back. And I'm sure she'll get in touch."

Lying beside her on the bed, I was not comforted by her words or her touch.

That evening, standing on the porch as my mother dozed inside, I looked at the steeples of St. Jude's Church rising above the treetops. A huge stone cross at the top of the highest steeple seemed to touch the sky. No one walked the street below, and no cars passed. It seemed as if everyone had gone away, and all the houses were vacant, the rooms occupied by ghosts. Of all the lonely towns we had lived in, Frenchtown was the loneliest.

————◦◦◦————

Two weeks later school started, and Kathleen Mary was still gone. I walked by her house after classes and paused, looked at the blank windows and the deserted porch, and then quickly walked away. Foolishly I had hoped her family might have returned.

Although she was probably far from French-town, her voice echoed in my ears, and the image of her blazing hair and green eyes often came into my mind. I began to hold silent conversations with her, the way I had often talked to Shirley Temple.

I scolded her for leaving me without any warning and for not getting in touch with me since then. I also defended her, considered that she must be living in desperate circumstances, which prevented her from sending a message. Perhaps she had been struck by her father during that last Frenchtown rampage and was lying somewhere in a hospital. This softened my attitude toward her, although I was angry because of the burden she had placed upon me.

"What burden?" I could hear her ask in that pert and sassy voice.

All this Catholic stuff. Not eating meat on Friday.

71

All the things Catholics are supposed to do. Going to mass on Sunday. Confession and communion. If I were a Catholic, I would have to do those things, wouldn't I?

But you're not a Catholic, are you?

Of course not. And I have no intention of becoming one.

Well, then, what's bothering you so much?

How I longed for Shirley Temple to be back in my life. Shirley and I'd never talked about religion or Catholics and Protestants or not eating meat on Friday. We'd chatted about what kind of outfits we'd wear that day, and I told her stories about cowboys galloping over the plains to rescue beautiful ladies from villains who always wore black. Sometimes I read page after page of my Green Gables books aloud to her.

Again I could hear Kathleen Mary taunting me: "Yes, but you're eleven now, going on twelve, too old to hold conversations with a doll."

In September at Mechanic Street School I took up my sixth-grade studies gratefully, concentrating, applying myself, filling my head with history and geography and arithmetic, all those facts and figures, so that there'd be room for nothing else.

No letter came from Kathleen Mary, and the letters from my father did not arrive very often. After a while I ignored the mail, remained in the house instead of watching for the mailman. Homework consumed me, and I was conscientious about performing the chores my mother left me to do.

I made no new friends at school, kept to myself at recess, reading in a quiet corner of the school yard. I remembered advice my father gave me when we moved to a new town: "If you find yourself on a strange street, don't make eye contact with anybody." I followed that advice at school, became expert at avoiding other people's eyes, and nobody sought me out. I did not want another friend. Did not need one. I tried not to think about Kathleen Mary, the same way I tried to banish my father and the dangers he faced, from my thoughts although they hovered at the edges of my mind. But each time I saw the steeples of St. Jude's, I could not stop thinking of her.

❖❖❖

Although the church steeples were a familiar sight, visible from almost every street in Frenchtown, the church itself, as big as a cathedral, remained remote and mysterious, cold gray stone and windows of orange glass—"They don't have enough money to buy stained-glass windows," Kathleen

Mary, who knew everything, once explained to me. Massive oak doors faced Mechanic Street, and stone angels guarded the entrance.

One day as I walked by the church, the sound of organ music came through the half-opened windows above the front entrance. Majestic music throbbed in the air followed by sweet strains, plaintive and delicate. I thought of my father and wondered how long it had been since he had heard music, and I stood there listening as he would listen, head tilted to one side, eyes half-closed.

I looked around to see if anyone was watching me. The few people on the street did not pay me any attention. The music continued, slowly building to a crescendo. I could hear Kathleen Mary saying, "Let's go inside," as if she were with me. Another of her adventures. I went up the stone steps and pulled open the heavy door, surrounded by the music. Stepping into the vestibule, I saw that the interior doors leading to the church were open. A big altar, like a huge white bedroom bureau, stood on a platform at the far end of the church, tall candles at either side of it. The steps of the platform were covered with dark red velvet. A huge wooden cross holding the crucified body of Jesus Christ dangled from the high, vaulted ceiling.

As I stepped into the church itself, the sun burst

through the windows, and it was like standing inside an exploding orange. The organ music was like thunder, so loud that I did not hear my footsteps as I walked up the aisle, awed by the height of the vaulted ceiling, the hanging chandeliers with bulbs shaped like candle flames. Plaques lined the walls depicting scenes from the life of Christ. Smaller statues of saints stood in grottoes on each side of the big altar. The air was faintly spicy with the smell of incense and melting wax, the aroma of holiness. The organ suddenly fell silent, although echoes of its strains lingered in my ears. I looked up at the choir loft, afraid that my presence had been discovered and I would be recognized as an impostor.

Nothing happened. Boldly, emulating Kathleen Mary, I slid into a pew and knelt down, which seemed the proper thing to do in a church. My eyes having become accustomed to the blazing light, I saw a woman bowed in prayer, a black shawl covering her head and shoulders. An old man moved down the aisle, pausing briefly before each plaque, head bowed, and then shuffled to the next one, his lips moving in silent prayer.

I, too, bowed my head and closed my eyes. I searched for the word to describe the church or myself at that moment. Serene? Maybe, because a kind of serenity seemed to have descended upon me. Or was it simply the deep silence after the thunder of the organ? After a few minutes I slipped out of the pew and walked almost on tiptoe down the aisle to the vestibule. It was dim after the brightness inside. Two bowls of holy water stood on slender pedestals on either side of the door, smaller and more modest than the basins at St. Brendan's but marble just the same. I dipped my right hand into the bowl, touched the tips of my fingers to the cool water, and made the sign of the cross. Stood there for a moment, waiting. I did not know what I was waiting for. The organ struck up again, music booming through the church, trembling the walls, blazing in the air.

The massive front door drew open, a slant of daylight spilled into the vestibule, and the shadow of an approaching figure fell across the floor. A woman of my mother's age stepped inside, her face arranged in an expression of piety, a brown felt hat plopped on her head, a red feather springing from the hat as if it would fly away.

A hat.

I had entered St. Jude's Roman Catholic Church without a hat on my head.

Was that a sin?

The woman looked directly at me, one arched eyebrow disappearing into a lock of hair on her forehead.

Before she could make an accusation, I got out of there, relieved when the big door closed behind me.

Going down the stone steps, catching my breath, I felt as though I had just returned from a journey to a foreign country and had been gone a long, long time.

If I were a Catholic, would I have to confess that I had gone into St. Jude's Church without a hat on my head?

❖❖❖

Hamburg sizzled on my plate, the patty surrounded by mashed potatoes and canned peas, swirling in a golden puddle of butter.

Ravenous, I watched my mother add small boiled onions to my plate. She had saved up her stamps for the meat and had also stood in line for an hour to purchase a pound of butter.

Before going to work that morning my mother had made an announcement. "Today is payday, Darcy," she said, combing her hair. "We are going to celebrate—I think your father would want us to." We did not maintain a silence about my father anymore but mentioned him often. Otherwise it would make it seem as if he were dead, my mother said. "So, hamburg for supper tonight and then to the Plymouth. Tyrone Power in *Crash Dive.*" She did not like action movies, but Tyrone Power was her favorite movie star.

Going to the Plymouth at night was always a thrill, made me feel older than eleven. The bonus was hamburg with mashed potatoes and peas, my favorite dinner. I vowed that when I grew up and married, I would choose a man who also loved hamburg and we would eat it every day of our lives, even on Thanksgiving Day and Christmas.

"Friday," my mother said gratefully as she sat down. "A day off tomorrow."

Friday. The word hung in the air as I lifted a forkful of hamburg to my lips. *Catholics don't eat meat on Friday.* As if Kathleen Mary's voice were whispering in my ear.

"What happens if Catholics eat meat on Friday?" I had asked her.

"First, it's a sin. You could be doomed to hell forever if you died with that sin on your soul. You have to confess it to be saved. Confessing a sin like that would also bring on a huge penance."

All those words dazzled me. Penance? But I did not ask about penance as Kathleen Mary continued, "Terrible things can happen if a Catholic eats meat on Friday. My father told us about a man at the comb shop. He brought a ham sandwich to work and it was Friday. He was a Catholic but a bad one. Know what he did?" Kathleen Mary paused dramatically. "He crammed his mouth with the ham sandwich and said,

'Let's see what God thinks of *that*.' " She paused again and then let me have it: "He choked to death. On the spot. Turned black and blue. And died right there."

I stared at the forkful of hamburg so close to my mouth that my eyes crossed as I looked at it. I lowered the fork and slid the piece of hamburg onto the plate. I took huge bites of mashed potatoes mixed with the peas. Chewing desperately because I was starved, I saw bits of meat in the gravy. Stalling, I cut the patty into squares and then even smaller squares.

I did not want to choke to death.

But I'm not even Catholic, I told myself.

"What's the matter?" my mother asked.

"Nothing," I said, my voice small.

"You're not eating," she said. "You haven't touched your hamburg. Don't you feel well?"

Without realizing it, she had presented me with a possible solution. "I guess I don't," I said.

Crestfallen, she said, "Your favorite supper—and all those stamps—Mr. Lucier ground that hamburg fresh for me."

Leaning across the table, she placed her hand on my forehead, letting it rest there for a moment. "You *do* feel a bit warm," she said. "Maybe you're coming down with something."

That was her favorite diagnosis, whether I

coughed a bit or sneezed or felt depressed or sniffled, or lost my appetite. *Coming down with something.*

I arranged my face to look as if I *might* be coming down with something, grateful for her diagnosis. At the same time I was dismayed. Disgusted in fact. Because I was hungry and a hamburg supper was my favorite meal and the sight of the patty and the smell of it and the onions and the sight of butter melting on the peas only increased my hunger.

Why don't you simply pick up the fork, load it with hamburg, put it in your mouth and eat it? I asked myself. How could I possibly choke to death if I wasn't a Catholic? Protestants were allowed to eat meat on Friday. I had been eating meat on Friday, especially hamburg, my entire life. It would not be a sin for me to do it. I would not choke to death. No matter what Kathleen Mary had done. People were not turned into Catholics by friends who talked some mumbo jumbo and sprinkled them with water from a marble basin. The basin was not even in the church but in the vestibule.

"I think I'll lie down for a while," I said. Funny, but suddenly I did not feel too well, felt as though I was actually coming down with something. Stop this, I scolded. Your imagination is running wild again.

"Maybe you'd better," my mother said, eyes soft with concern. "Poor Darcy."

In my bedroom, lonesome as I glanced at the place on my bureau where Shirley Temple once looked down on me, I pulled the bedspread up to my chin. It must be terrible to choke to death, I thought, and sighed with relief at my close call, my escape from the table. I shut my eyes, in case my mother peeked into the room. I also knew that it was necessary for me to make a remarkable recovery in time for that Tyrone Power movie.

Eyes closed, hands languishing at my sides, I drifted dreamily until a sudden thought pushed its way to my consciousness:

What would I do next Friday?

And all the Fridays to come?

———❖❖❖———

"Mom, how do people become Catholic?"

"Well, they're born that way, I guess."

"I mean, how do they become Catholic if they aren't born that way?"

My mother paused, reflecting, half-closing her eyes, which she always did when she was deep in thought. She also put down the *Woman's Home Companion* she was reading.

"Well, they become converts."

The word was vaguely familiar, and I searched

my memory for conversations with Kathleen Mary for a definition of the word and found none.

"If somebody wants to become a Catholic," she said, "they go visit a priest and ask him for directions. Wait a minute, instructions, I think they call it. And the priest gives them instructions on how to become a Catholic."

"And what are those instructions?" I persisted.

"Know what, Darcy? This reminds me of when you were, oh, about three years old and asked question after question about, it seems, everything in the universe. And every time I answered a question, you asked another one. 'Why?' That's what you'd say: 'Why?' There was no end to it." She laughed tenderly, tousled my hair, and picked up the magazine again.

So. To become a convert, I would have to see a priest.

But why would I go see a priest?

First of all I didn't want to become a Catholic, with all that Latin hocus-pocus, mass every Sunday, winter and summer, all during vacations. I didn't want to give up meat forever on Friday. How about confession and communion? Hey, that's right, how *about* confession and communion? I tried to remember all the information Kathleen Mary had dispensed about her religion, but the rules and regulations were all jumbled in my mind. For instance not wearing a hat in church? How could that possibly be a sin? The Ten Commandments said nothing about wearing a hat in church.

"Mom?" I said.

She placed the magazine on her lap and looked at me with *that look,* the look that said, "Yes, Darcy, I am trying to appear interested, but I would also like to finish this story."

"Yes, hon?" she said. Funny, *hon* is usually a term of endearment, but when she said *hon* instead of *Darcy,* I knew that her patience was coming to an end.

"Are all religions equal?"

"I'm not sure what you mean by that." One finger holding her place in the magazine.

"I mean, does God really care if you're Protestant, like Unitarian, or Catholic?"

She did not answer immediately but continued to gaze at me, curiously. "God doesn't care, Darcy. Or at least nobody ever told me he does. If you try to be a good person, try to keep in touch with him, keep the Commandments, then I don't think it matters if you are Unitarian or Jewish or Catholic."

Pondering this information, which made a great deal of sense and cheered me up, I nodded and began to turn away.

"Darcy," she said.

Her voice stopped me, and I turned back.

She closed her magazine and beckoned me to her. Took my hands and drew me close until I could see the tiny pores in her cheeks.

"Now, what's this all about?"

That was the moment when I should have told her about the terrible thing Kathleen Mary had done, remembering the touch of holy water on my head and cheeks: "I think Kathleen Mary made me a Catholic." The words sounded ridiculous in my mind, and I knew they would sound even more ridiculous if I spoke them out loud. Because Kathleen Mary O'Hara had not made me a Catholic. My mother's words had made that plain. To become a convert, you had to seek instructions from a priest. You needed more than a few words of mumbo jumbo chanted by a girl your own age while she tossed a few drops of water around the place.

"Oh, nothing," I said. "Just curious. Something I was reading in a book."

"Don't tell me Anne of Green Gables wants to become a Catholic."

We both laughed, and my mother, to my intense relief, opened her magazine and I was given my freedom from her interrogation.

One thing was clear: God didn't care whether you were a Catholic or not. If he didn't care, why should I worry about it?

———✥✥✥———

The next afternoon I saw the people running. They were running along Mechanic Street, streaming from their houses, down the steps, and onto the sidewalks. Sirens pierced the air, those terrible sounds of emergency, distant at first, then drawing nearer, louder, and finally the roaring of the fire engines as they streaked by, hectic red, bells clanging, long ladders bouncing, and firemen clinging to the brass rails, their black rubber coats flapping behind them.

Returning from Lucier's Market, where I seemed to spend half my life buying groceries, I had been disappointed because no meat was available and I had to settle for mackerel, which did not require ration stamps but was bony and oily-tasting. But my disappointment was forgotten when the people started running and the fire trucks went by.

I looked toward the corner of Mechanic and Fifth streets where a crowd was beginning to gather, and I began to run, too, glad for a bit of excitement after a dull, routine day at school. Turning the corner onto Fifth Street, I saw the cause of the excitement. The eyes of the crowd were fixed on the top floor of a three-decker, where a young woman stood precariously on the porch banister, one hand holding on to a post which anchored a clothesline that stretched across space to the house next door. Firemen were raising a tall ladder into the air and calling up to her. A policeman stood on the hood of a black cruiser, hands cupped around his mouth. "Don't move," he pleaded. "We will help you."

The woman stared down at the firemen and the policeman and the crowd, a puzzled expression on her face, as if she was wondering what we were all doing there. I took off my glasses, which were smudged as usual, and wiped them on the hem of my skirt. Putting them on once more, squinting to see her more clearly, I realized that there was something familiar about her. I had seen that face before. Her expression had now changed from bewilderment to one I could not pin down, although this, too, was faintly familiar. Haunted, that was it. A haunted look, like the one on the face of the young woman who had knelt in front of Sister Angela in the convent courtyard. I studied her further as she began to sway on the banister, and all doubts were banished. This was the same young woman. The crowd came alive to me then as if I had been deaf or in a world of my own for those few moments.

The crowd was shouting at her.

"Don't jump, Mimi."

"Hold on, hold on."

And other shouts in French that I did not understand, although I knew the meaning of the words,
pleading with her not to jump.

"Poor girl, poor Mimi," said a middle-aged
woman nearby, a big woman with gray-streaked hair
pulled back into a bun, tears rolling down her cheeks.
She pressed a handkerchief to her mouth.

The firemen were encountering difficulty raising the ladder, having trouble with the extension
that would allow them to reach that third floor.
Meanwhile a fireman in a black rubber coat and hel-
met appeared on the porch, a few feet from the
young woman. She glanced at him, puzzled, then
frightened, spoke to him, words we could not hear.
The fireman removed his hat, revealing blond, curly
hair, a young face, barely older than the troubled girl
herself. He raised his hands in an attitude of pleading, the drama of the porch causing silence to fall in
the crowd, all faces still upraised.

"Don't come closer, or I'll jump," the girl called,
her words clear and distinct in the silence.

As she spoke, she lost her balance, swaying dan-
gerously, standing on one leg, the other swinging
wildly in the air. She clutched the post with her
hands, both feet on the rail of the banister again, and
the crowd sighed with relief, as if the crowd had
suddenly become one person.

And then a chorus of voices filled the air, calling,
"Mimi . . . Mimi . . . ," and the young woman
named Mimi looked down, still bewildered, as if she
did not know who Mimi was, knees wobbling, one
hand outstretched, the other barely holding on to the
post. The young fireman continued to talk to her, but
she paid him no attention and he stepped closer.

On the ground the struggle continued with the
ladder, and now another truck arrived, screeching to
a halt, men leaping from the vehicle even before it
stopped.

As the girl continued to stare down at the crowd,
a group of firemen from the newly arrived truck
rushed forward, unfolding a giant net, grappling
with it desperately.

I wanted to leave, to go home, anywhere, but
could not, hopelessly pinned to that spot in the
crowd. My heart pounded, the smell of the fish in the
package sickened me, and I felt vomit gathering in
my throat. I choked it down. Pain gripped my neck as
I gazed upward and my glasses slipped down my
nose. I reached up to push them back and saw her
step off the banister.

She did not jump but simply took a step into
space and then another, her skirt suddenly flaring
out and her legs walking on nothing. She fell, arms
flung outward so that she seemed like a living cross,

but only for a fraction of a second. Her fall was swift. She was in the air and suddenly not there, and a sound emerged from the crowd that was like no other sound on earth, a cry of anguish and astonishment and then another sound, flesh meeting pavement, bone against cement, a squashing, terrible sound that made me turn away, made me bolt through the crowd, flinging myself through the forest of arms and legs, scurrying frantically, my sobs soundless in my ears because the cries and moans of the crowd robbed them from me, although the tears on my cheeks were my own.

Emerging from the crowd, standing at the corner, catching my breath, wiping my tears with the backs of my hands, I did not know what to do. Or where to go. I wanted to hide but did not know where I could hide or who I would be hiding from.

Minutes later, out of breath, tears on my cheeks, I passed by St. Jude's Church, then the school, then the convent. I did not pause to look at the convent but quickened my step, wishing that I could confront Kathleen Mary O'Hara at this moment and tell her that her Catholic religion was a fake, that miracles do not occur, that old Sister Angela was a fraud, unable to save a young woman from killing herself.

"Thank God I'm not a Catholic," I said, without knowing whether I spoke aloud or silently. And ran the rest of the way home.

———✦✦✦———

My mother did not know that I had witnessed the death of the girl whose name, I learned, was Michele Tourneau, and I pretended a lack of interest when she reported stories that had circulated in the factory about the girl. She had been despondent for months, my mother said at the supper table, and had been under treatment by a psychiatrist in Worcester.

Focusing on my plate although the food did not appeal to me, I listened intently, wanting to hear all the details but asking no questions and making no comments, afraid that my mother would somehow figure out that I had been at the scene. I also feared that someone she worked with might have seen me on Fifth Street that day.

I did not want my mother to know what I had seen because she had always protected me from the terrible things going on in the world. Sarah Stone, one of my classmates in Clapham, North Carolina, had been killed when she fell off a trolley car, and my mother would not let me go to the wake, even though my classmates attended in a body, marching into the funeral home together. "I want you to remember Sarah as you knew her, Darcy, not laid out in a coffin," she had said.

"They say that mental problems run in Mimi Tourneau's family," my mother continued. "One of her uncles threw himself in front of a train out in Arkansas a few years ago. He was a hobo."

My curiosity betrayed the silence I had vowed to maintain: "Did she leave a note?"

"No, but they said she tried to do it earlier. Took some pills, which only made her sick. Poor kid. She must have been very sad, very desperate to do a thing like that. And no one to help her."

Not even Sister Angela and her miracles, I thought.

That night I dreamed of Mimi Tourneau. All dressed in white, she stood at the edge of deep woods, her eyes closed, her face in sweet repose. Then her face changed, her mouth opened, her hair flared out as if swept by strong winds, and her eyes opened, not eyes really but blank spaces. Her mouth was also a blank space, and from it came a voice calling for help, a child's desperate cry, and as I tried to raise my hands to my ears to blot out her cries, her voice changed and so did her face, and now it was not her face at all but another emerging from her own, my father's face, sad and lost, and his own voice replacing hers, and he was pleading now for help, calling across time and space, and I leapt into wakefulness, clutching my pillow in terror, my own voice caught in a silent scream. "Daddy, Daddy," I whispered quietly in the night, my terror replaced after a while by sadness and longing and loneliness. I lay awake for a long time, listening to the night noises, thankful that I did not hear voices calling to me.

The next day my mother received a telegram from the U.S. Department of War informing her that my father was missing in action somewhere in the European Theater of Operations.

*M*issing in Action.

Lying in bed at night, I tried to conjure up the meaning of those words. "Another way of saying lost," my mother said. I envisioned my father wandering deserted battlefields alone, wounded, dazed, trying to find his way through shelled and abandoned towns, not knowing his name, not remembering my mother's name or mine—and I leapt from the bed to escape the nightmare. But this was not a nightmare or a dream, this was real life, the light from a streetlamp slanting into the room, turning the draperies into pale ghosts. You can escape a dream or nightmare by waking up, but what do you do when you are already awake and the nightmare continues?

"He may be a prisoner of war," my mother said the next day in an effort to console us both. "Healthy and not wounded at all."

"POWs get proper care," said Mr. LeBlanc downstairs. His words curled with a gentle French accent. As a foreman at the Lucite plant, he had spoken for my mother when she applied for a job. He was so polite that he did not get a moment's rest, always opening doors, holding a chair when someone sat down, leaping to his feet when a visitor arrived, constantly offering refreshments and food. He also offered my mother and me consolation as we sat on his porch in the evening. "The rules of war say that prisoners must be treated with respect. Even the Nazis do that," he said. And leapt to his feet to serve us more lemonade.

My father, a prisoner. In a drab uniform. In handcuffs maybe or chains. I recalled the gaunt, hopeless faces of war prisoners in the newsreels, sunken eyes and hollow cheeks. My wistful father, without his hidden bottle to keep his spirits up, at the mercy of Storm Troopers. Tortured perhaps for information about the location of bridges.

Sitting on the porch in the coolness of October evenings, my mother and I were seldom alone. Mr. and Mrs. LeBlanc visited us almost nightly, bringing something to eat—all sorts of pies made of rhubarb or blueberries or strawberries that Mrs. LeBlanc had canned back in the summertime. She was a big, vigorous woman who did not speak English, and Mr. LeBlanc acted as her interpreter.

The Lombard sisters from upstairs did not visit us but knocked at our door once or twice a week and presented us with delicacies—butterscotch drops and caramel—tasty candies called *belango* and clusters of meringue dipped in honey. They were too shy to speak and they never lingered at the door but hurried back up the stairs to their tenement. Armand Pottier next door, whom Mr. LeBlanc said left the seminary after years of study for the priesthood, brought us a small wooden cross he had carved from the branch of a cherry tree. He was tall and thin and mournful-looking.

"God is chasing him," Mr. LeBlanc said, "but he won't give in."

"Does God really chase people?" I asked, astonished at the prospect.

"If you have a vocation and you resist, as Armand Pottier did, God will not let you go," he said. Frowning, he added, "Of course maybe God didn't want him for a priest in the first place. Then he was right to come out. Either way he's a sad man."

What a strange God these Catholics have, I thought, who chases people.

"Mrs. LeBlanc wants you to know that we pray every night for your husband," Mr. LeBlanc said in his formal way when they left one evening. "And light candles in church on Sunday."

I tried to pray for my father. Knelt beside my bed at night, my hands clasped together. I had always said my prayers tucked securely in bed, that simple supplication, "Now I lay me down to sleep," and then asking God to keep my mother and father safe and to help all the poor people of the world. Kathleen Mary said that prayers on your knees rose more quickly to heaven. I doubted the truth of that but knelt anyway, not wanting to take any chances with my father's safety. I added the "Our Father" to my prayers, closing my eyes, concentrating. But the prayers seem to be only words, nothing more. What was missing? I thought of all the terrible things going on in the war, all that God allowed to happen. I thought of my father lost somewhere. And poor Mimi Tourneau, for whom there had been no miracle. I did not know how to pray properly, but even if I did, would God listen? But I still knelt down every night and said my prayers, even though I doubted that God could possibly hear me from a three-decker tenement in Frenchtown, Massachusetts.

———❖❖❖———

U.S. Army General Hospital
Fort Hobart, Kansas
Dear Mrs. Webster:

I have been wanting to write to you for some time but was unable to do so because my right hand has been disabled and I have only recently regained the use of it. I have been here at Hobart General for three weeks and am being treated very well.

I am writing because your husband, Bill, and I served together in the 116th Engineers. Bill is a fine man, a real gentleman, and I consider him a good friend. The reason why I am writing this letter is to tell you that Bill is a true hero. He saved my life. I would not be alive today if it weren't for him.

I can't tell you in great detail what happened, but let me say that it was action near a bridge that we had worked on behind enemy lines deep inside ———. We were being bombed extensively from the air and shelled from enemy positions a few miles away. Bill and I ran for protection under the bridge, when a bomb exploded nearby, pinning me down.

Bill could easily have left me there, and it would have been understandable. In fact there was so much confusion and so much

97

smoke and fire that I thought that I was a goner. The upper part of my body and my right arm were pinned under a block of concrete. Bill suddenly appeared out of the smoke and flames. He was limping. He had a gash on his forehead. Somehow he was able to free me. How he moved that huge piece of concrete is beyond my understanding. But he did it while all the time, bombs were falling and rocks were tumbling around us.

Just as he set me free, a series of explosions occurred close by. We were thrown apart from each other. I lost consciousness. When I woke up, I was in an airplane on my way back to our headquarters.

There is no doubt in my mind that I would have died beneath that bridge if Bill had not stopped and set me free, at the risk of his own life.

I know that Bill has been reported missing in action, but I feel in my heart that he is safe. The ——— Resistance is very active in the area where that action took place, and it's my belief that he was rescued by them and is now being hidden until they can make contact with our troops. This has happened in other cases.

Please take heart from these words of mine.

I hope you and your daughter, Darcy, are doing fine. Bill and I talked a lot about our families. Before joining the army, I worked for the Post Office in my home town, Dirksen, Missouri. I am married to my high school sweetheart, Janet, and we have two children, twins, a boy and a girl, Richie and Ruthie. I am going home on furlough next week to see them.

I must close now, as my hand is beginning to tire a bit. Please take courage from this letter. I feel in my bones that Bill is safe.

Say hello to Darcy and tell her how much her father missed her and how much he loved both of you.

Very truly yours,
Vernon Hastings (Sergeant First Class)

My mother sat alone on the porch, the letter from Sgt. Vernon Hastings on her lap. She had been sitting there for more than an hour, staring into space and occasionally reading the letter again. Standing at

Standing at the kitchen door not knowing what to do, whether to join her on the porch or stay inside, I waited hoping she would call me and hoping also that she would not call me.

the kitchen door, not knowing what to do, whether to join her on the porch or stay inside, I waited, hoping she would call me to her and hoping also that she would not call me. So I stood there, quiet, counting seconds then minutes as twilight crept across the neighborhood, blunting the sharp edges of things.

I thought of my father and his heroic deed and how proud I had been as my mother and I read the letter together. Her eyes had been brimming with pride and happiness as she reached to hug me.

"Your father's a real war hero," my mother had said. "Is there anything greater than saving someone's life at the risk of your own?"

"I'll bet he'll receive a medal," I said. "Maybe the Silver Star." I did not know what a serviceman had to do to earn a Silver Star, but I knew it was awarded for the performance of heroic deeds.

We then read the letter again, carefully, savoring each word.

"I hate to think of him in all that bombing," she said, pausing once. "Here we are, safe and sound, and he was in so much danger."

We continued reading silently, and that was when I saw the word. Had passed over it before in that first quick reading but saw it vividly now. That terrible past tense of a word. The room seemed to sway, the walls lurching, the floor buckling under the sofa. I looked away, blinking to make the room settle down, wondering if my mother had seen the word too. Then I felt her stiffen. Wait, can you feel some-one stiffen? Yet she changed, became different, yes, stiffened as she sat beside me. And at the same time she seemed to withdraw, to go away, the way my father used to become remote. I knew then that she had seen the word.

I leapt up to wipe the dishes, almost dropped her favorite cup, real bone china, white with a red rose on the inside of the cup. My fingers were clumsy, my hands shaking.

Finally the dishes were done and put away. Never had they rattled so much as I placed them on the shelves, never had I come so close to dropping not only her favorite cup but two glasses as well.

That word.

That damn word, I thought, and felt instantly guilty for swearing like that.

Loved.

Sgt. Hastings had written: *how much he loved both of you.* Loved, the past tense of love. Which means he thought my father was past tense too. A slip of the lip, but can you call it a slip of the lip when it appears in a letter?

So, despite all his reassurances and what he claimed was his belief in my father's safety, he had betrayed himself with that terrible word, *loved,* and did not even notice it.

Now my mother sat on the porch, in the shadows, not moving, and I waited inside, standing in the doorway. After a while I went to my room. Did not want to stay in my room—why did I ever give Shirley Temple away?—yet did not want to sit with my mother, afraid of what she might say. As long as I did not talk to her, there was a possibility that she had not noticed the word. But of course she had. Why didn't she say something? Why didn't she talk to me about it? And I realized that maybe she thought I hadn't seen it and wanted to protect me from that knowledge.

Or was I making too much of that one small word in the first place?

But it was not only the word. Once the betrayal of that past tense had been revealed, his entire letter read differently, full of false bravado, brave sentences but all of them empty and hollow.

"Darcy."

I realized she had been calling my name, once or twice, maybe three times.

Trudging through the kitchen and the back hallway, I arrived at the porch, still in that in-between state—wanting to be with her and not wanting to be.

She patted the cushion next to her on the bench. When I was seated, she said, "Yes, Darcy, I saw it too. That tiny mistake Sergeant Hastings made . . ."

I was about to speak to assure her that it had to be a mistake, a natural error anyone could make.

"Shh, don't say anything, Darcy," she whispered. "I've been sitting here thinking and I realize that we have to be positive. We have to *believe*. We have to believe your father is safe. That he'll be found. That he'll come home. And he'll hug us both."

We hugged each other then, caught up in that vision of my father returning home, safe and sound. She held me so tightly that her fingernails dug into the flesh of my arms, and the next day I saw the red indentations.

We have to believe your father is safe, she had said.

But she did not believe it. Instead she thought that my father, her husband, was dead. I knew that's what she believed, because my mother, from that moment on, grew very still.

October that year was crisp and golden, sunlight streaming through scarlet leaves and the clanging of horseshoes in the long evenings as the shadows lengthened. In the empty lot across the street from our three-decker, men gathered every night after supper and threw horseshoes while spectators cheered or applauded or whooped and laughed, metal striking metal and a cry of "Ringer, Ringer" echoing in the air. The women sat patiently on the sidelines, and the children ran wild and played their own mysterious games.

My mother and I watched from our porch, my mother in her stillness, sitting next to me but somehow miles away, as if in another time and place. Yes, she talked, answered my questions, prepared our meals, spoke about her work at the shop (the new batch of Lucite that had to be rejected because it refused to stiffen), but despite all these outward signs that all was normal, there was a part of her that I could not reach or touch. A quietness, as if she had retreated to a safe place and in that safe place she was unreachable.

"Mom, are you all right?" I asked.

Not once but many times, although rationing the times I asked the question so that she would not grow impatient and shut me off completely.

"Of course," she'd say brightly, but a headache brightness in her eyes, her voice half an octave too high.

She worked at the shop and supervised my homework, helping me with the difficult arithmetic problems—arithmetic, always my doom, my scholastic tragedy—and hemmed my dresses and knitted mittens for the approaching winter, but always merely going through the motions, almost mechanical. Push a button: *Hi, Darcy, how are you today?* Push another: *It's warm for October, isn't it.* Push another: *Time for bed, Darcy.*

When she returned from work, she did not ask, "Any letter today, Darcy?" She expected none. How could a dead soldier write a letter? I tried to pray at night on my knees, but my thoughts were jumbled and the words of the prayers meaningless. I could not believe that my father was dead. I tried to picture him alive, in a hospital somewhere, under the care of doctors and nurses. But the vision dissolved when that terrible sentence reverberated in my mind: *how much he loved both of you. Loved.* He can't love you any longer because he is no longer alive. I tried to flee from the thoughts, but there was no place to go, not even my mother's room next door to mine, so near to me and yet more distant than the stars and planets.

My mother spent long hours in her bedroom, damp towels on her forehead. She would awaken and stalk to the kitchen, gulping more pills, smiling wanly at me, patting my head absently, speaking only when I pushed those verbal buttons.

The stillness in her frightened me.

Because I knew what the stillness meant.

It meant that part of her had died, too, along with my father.

One day after classes, lugging my heavy schoolbag loaded with books, I took the long way home, delaying the moment when I would face again a mailbox without any letters at all and an empty tenement, my mother still at work and somehow absent even when she was home.

Trudging along Seventh Street, I was disgusted with the names of the streets. All those numbers. Why not beautiful names like Vista Drive and Blossom Avenue and Rosebud Lane? Instead First and Second streets and all the other numbers plus Mechanic Street. Ugh! What had prompted someone to choose a name like Mechanic Street?

As I walked slowly along Seventh, head down, impeded by the weight of my schoolbag, a small orange ball bounced in front of me and dribbled into the gutter. Looking up, I saw a child, perhaps three years old, standing below the steps of a white bunga- low with green shutters.

Sighing wearily, in no mood to be playing games with a child, I slung my schoolbag over my shoulder and retrieved the ball. Balancing it on one palm, I turned and looked at her.

I recognized her immediately and stood open- mouthed in my surprise.

"Ball, ball," she cried, holding out her hands. "Throw ball."

"Here you are," I said, tossing it gently to her. She missed it, and the ball dropped at her feet as she laughed, the high, giggling laughter of a little girl.

"Pick it up, Monique," a woman called from the porch, only a few feet away across a patch of carefully tended lawn. One-story bungalows were not com- mon in Frenchtown, although the French Canadians carefully tended their patches of lawn, however small.

The child picked up the ball and held it in front of her, inspecting it seriously, as if she had never seen a ball before.

I could not believe my eyes.

I looked up at the mother and recognized her as

well—although her hair was shorter than when I had last seen her with Kathleen Mary, in the courtyard of the convent, when she had stood before Sister Angela on that long-ago afternoon.

I began to ask, "Where are her braces?" but stopped myself.

"She's beautiful," I said, wondering what had happened to rid the child of her braces, not daring to believe what I believed might have happened.

"Thank you," the woman said. "She's a good girl."

"How old is she?" Tossing the ball to the child again and the child dropping it again, the ball rolling away from her as she giggled with delight.

"Three and a half," she said.

"She looks very healthy."

I could not believe I had said those words. Who says that about a child? You say a lot of things, how beautiful they are or how smart or how polite or a thousand other things but not "She looks very healthy." Not unless you are fishing for information. Which is exactly what I was doing.

"She's a brave little girl," her mother said. "She's had a hard life."

"Oh." Hoping that my face looked innocent, I asked, "Has she been sick?"

"Crippled, since she was born," she said, the light Canuck accent curling her words as if each sentence were a question and not a statement. "Bone disease, the doctors did not know the cause. Poor Monique, she learned to walk with braces."

It was impossible for me to resist asking the next question. "Did the doctors finally find a cure?"

"Not the doctors," she said. "A miracle saved her."

I stood still, my arms at my sides. The child threw the ball at me, but I did not try to catch it. It bounced down the sidewalk to a telephone pole. I did not retrieve it, waiting for her mother to speak.

"Sister Angela, at the convent." Again the gentle accent with the curl. "She blessed her, prayed for her. Exactly one week later, almost to the minute, she was cured. A miracle."

Tears filled my eyes as I turned to retrieve the ball. After picking it up, I walked back and tossed the ball at the child, who squealed with pure pleasure as, this time, she caught it.

"Look at her," the mother said. "See what God can do. What Sister Angela can do with God's help."

The child held the ball delicately as if she were holding the world in her hands, the ball like a small globe.

"I'm so happy for you," I said, "for you and Monique."

As I made to leave, the child called, "Stay . . . stay . . ."

"She wants to play," the mother said. "Every minute, like making up for lost time."

"I have to go," I said, eager to be away, to ponder the miracle, to let my heart quiet down, my blood to stop pulsing so feverishly inside my veins. "But I'll come back."

The child waved to me, the orange ball in her hand.

The mother waved, her hand small and delicate like a pale bird.

$\mathcal{A}$s I made my way
through the puzzle of shrubbery that surrounded St.
Jude's convent, I hoped that I was not too late to find
Sister Angela in the courtyard.

All day long I had pondered whether to go to the
convent and speak to the old nun. How could I ask
her for a miracle when I was not a Catholic? Or did
Kathleen Mary somehow perform a miracle when
she sprinkled me with the holy water and I was now a
kind of Catholic? Or was I using that argument simply to make my request to Sister Angela legitimate?

Distracted, depressed, my usual Sunday blues, I

decided finally that my father's safety was worth more than my own embarrassment or disgrace or whatever would happen at the convent. Now I was afraid that I would be too late, that the old nun and all the people asking for miracles would be gone. I hurried through the avenues of hedges, falling once and scraping my knee. At last I arrived at the latticed courtyard. Pushing aside thick bushes, I looked through the openings of the fence and was grateful when I saw that Sister Angela was still there, sitting on the marble bench. She was alone, all the people gone, no other nuns in attendance.

She seemed to be nodding, sleeping perhaps, as the shadows grew long. The afternoon was warm like an August day misplaced in October, hazy sun now lowering in the west over the tenement roofs of Frenchtown.

Did I dare to wake her? To interrupt her rest? She must be very tired after having people visit her all day. All those prayers, all those favors being sought.

Maybe she heard me stirring in the bushes or had felt my approach to the fence, because suddenly she lifted her head, turned, and looked my way. Was she able to see me through the bushes and latticed fence? I stayed completely still, holding my breath.

She raised a tiny hand, rosary beads dangling from her fingers, and beckoned to me. Hesitating, feeling like a spy who has been discovered, I let my breath out, my heart beating so loudly I thought that she must be able to hear it.

She pointed to an opening at the end of the fence. Brushing against the fence and trying to avoid the bushes that tugged like stiff fingers at my dress, I made my way to the opening and slowly walked across the stone courtyard to stand in front of her.

Until this moment I had only caught glimpses of her face. She was old, all right, the flesh of her face almost transparent as if the years had worn away her skin the way rain will wear away even a stone. Her eyes, though, were bright blue, clear as water in a spring stream.

"Come, young miss," she said, making room on the bench. "Sit with me."

The English words surprised me. I had been prepared to explain my purpose in sign language, assisted by the few French words I had picked up from the LeBlancs downstairs. Had rehearsed, in fact, the words that would convey the reason for my visit. *Mon père* . . . my father . . . *perdu* . . . lost . . . *la guerre* . . . the war . . ."

Now shyness overcame me. But more than shyness, guilt and shame. Why hadn't I simply stood in line and joined the procession of people who had come before her with their problems?

"Now tell me, what is your name and what is troubling you?" she asked.

"My name is Darcy Webster," I said, "and I don't belong here. I'm not a Catholic." Then paused, responding to that gentle face and those understanding eyes. "At least I don't think I'm a Catholic. I'm supposed to be a Unitarian. My mother and father are Unitarians." I could not stop talking. Thought I had finished and then went on. "When they go to church, that is." Then fell into silence, blushing, feeling a fool, wishing I had not come.

"You don't think you are a Catholic?" she asked, seizing on the words I had tried to pass quickly over.

I told her then of Kathleen Mary and the visit to St. Brendan's and the holy water and the words that still rang in my ears: *Now you're a Catholic, Darcy Webster. Forever and ever, world without end, Amen.*

Again I couldn't stop talking: "And now I don't know whether I should eat meat on Friday, and I stopped in at church one day and didn't wear a hat, and I haven't been to confession . . ." Finally I stopped, out of breath, as if I'd been running fast, trying to catch up to Kathleen Mary.

The small nun shook her head, and she was so doll-like, her flesh so much like delicate porcelain, that I almost expected her to squeak the way Shirley Temple had squeaked when I'd moved her arms or turned her head.

"What about God, dear young Darcy?" she asked gently.

"What do you mean?"

"I mean, all this about meat on Friday and the rest, where does God come into it?"

Frowning, looking away to avoid those clear, penetrating eyes of hers, I realized that I had been so busy thinking about all the Catholic rules and regulations that I had not thought about God. And when I *did* think of God while trying to pray, he seemed out of reach, did not seem to exist for me in fact.

"God comes first, you see," she said. "Not whether you are this or that, Protestant or Catholic, young or old. Loving God is the first thing."

Who is he, really? I wondered. And why should I love him?

"You must love God because without him we are nothing," she said, as if I had spoken my doubts aloud. "God gave you life, gave your mother and father life. Gave them the love they have for each other, the love they have for you."

She touched my bare arm, her fingers as light as flower petals on my skin.

"Dear, dear Darcy," she said, "don't frown, don't be worried, don't be unhappy. God is letting you discover him. Meanwhile let the days bring you what they will and don't fuss or fret about who you are or what you are. Let the days come, the darkness and the light, and don't concern yourself."

Her words reminded me of what old Reverend Wilmot Deems had said, and I let them flow over me as I had in his church that Sunday. "God takes care of us all, whether you know it or not. He does it anyway. And if you pray to him, he will listen."

"But I don't know how to pray," I said. "I don't know any prayers, no real prayers, that is. Only 'Now I lay me down to sleep' and 'Our Father.'"

Smiling a bit, she said, "The words are not important. Prayer is reaching out, like a hand stretched out to God and the hand can reach across eternity. It has nothing to do with words."

We sat in silence for a few moments, the rosary beads entwined on her fingers, a bird fluttering in a tree nearby, the failing sun throwing shadows on the courtyard. A quiet place, like an oasis. After a while she said, "Now, Darcy Webster. Tell me what brought you here today."

"My father," I said. "He's in the army. He's missing in action. The other day I saw the little girl who came to you last summer. She wore braces on her legs." Once again my words went on and on, and I was powerless to stop them. "But when I saw her this week, the braces were gone. I played ball with her. She ran and jumped. Her mother said . . ." And now I faltered, words failing me finally.

"Her mother said it was a miracle." Sister Angela finished the sentence for me.

"Yes." Then the question popped out of my mouth, brazen and bold. "Was it a miracle?" I immediately wished the question back, unspoken.

"There are so many miracles every day," she said. "The sun rising and setting. Water that quenches our thirst. A child in pain and the pain ceases."

I thought of poor Mimi Tourneau, her terrible sadness, leaping to her death.

"But bad things still happen," I said. "Some people don't get cured, people suffer, they die. Why does God let that happen?"

"God, who gives us everything, can also take away everything," she said. "Why should we question what God does? He has his own design. He gives us so much, and he asks so little."

She took my hands in hers and draped the rosary beads around them, the touch of the wooden beads cool against my skin. She murmured words I did not understand, not French. Latin, no doubt, her voice a whisper. "For your father," she said, bowing, whispering the prayer again.

We seemed joined together in a bond that would never break, as if we were united forever, caught in a sweet silence so profound and lovely that I heard no

"Now, Darcy Webster. Tell me what brought you here today."

birds, no distant hum of traffic, no cries of children or barking dogs.

Is this what they mean by peace? I wondered.

My eyes opened. Our hands parted, and she gathered the rosary into the folds of her robe. I was conscious of a sudden chill in the air, the dimming sun, the lateness of the hour. I stood up. "I think I should go now, Sister."

"Go in peace, dear Darcy. Learn to see the miracles that surround you. Everything else will come . . . prayer and love . . ."

I paused, hesitating, wondering whether I dared to ask the question I burned to ask. Then thought, Why not? I felt nothing was too much for her.

"Are you a bride of Christ?" I asked, and immediately could have kicked myself for asking such a question.

She laughed, delicate laughter like a fountain splashing on a warm afternoon, and held up her left hand. For the first time I saw the gold band on the third finger.

"Yes, I am a bride of Christ," she said.

"But girls become brides when they fall in love and get married," I said, committed now to finding out all about nuns and God and Christ.

"Love is everywhere, Darcy, and knows no borders. All the different kinds of love. Between men and women, parents and children. God loves us and sent his son to us. Isn't it possible to fall in love with him? A different kind of love, perhaps, but love all the same."

I tried to grasp the meaning of it all but could not quite understand, like not understanding the lyrics of a song although the melody is clear and beautiful.

She seemed weary suddenly, her shoulders drooping, her eyes losing their luster.

"Thank you, Sister Angela, for everything."

The brightness came back to her eyes. "Someday, dear, dear Darcy, you will learn to pray and you will fall in love."

"May I visit you again?" I asked.

She smiled faintly. "I will not be here, dear girl. It is time for me to go. To go home." She brought a thin finger to her lips. "It is our secret, Darcy. Ours and God's." Perhaps she saw the sadness in my eyes as the meaning of her words became clear to me. "Be happy for me, Darcy."

She closed her eyes, her face in sweet repose, hands clasped together, the rosary beads entwined around her fingers. I waited there awhile as she slept on. Then I whispered good-bye and left, following the path Kathleen Mary had showed me through the puzzle of the shrubbery.

She died three days later. I stood in line to view her body at the convent. Her face was still in sweet repose, and the rosary beads were still entwined around her fingers.

———✧✧✧———

Through a mix-up in communications, my mother received the letter from Lt. Frederick Marcancio of Company E, 116th Division, U.S. Army Corps of Engineers the day before the official telegram arrived from the Department of War stating that my father was no longer listed as missing in action but was a patient at Longworth Hospital in Bristol, England.

Lieutenant Marcancio's letter read as follows:

Dear Mrs. Webster:

I am happy to be writing good news. Your husband, Bill, is on the road to recovery. He is sitting here with me as I write this letter. Yes, he is injured, but is doing quite well. He suffered fractures to both his elbows during an explosive attack on our positions in

————. His arms are in casts in upright positions. He cannot dress himself or eat without assistance. He can't write of course, and that's why I am writing this letter for him.

He was listed as missing in action because he was in a coma, first in a military hospital in —— and now here in Bristol. The explosion that injured him also tore off his dog tags and most of his clothes. He remained unidentified all the time he was in the coma but is now awake and normal. In fact he is grinning at me as I write this and will be dictating the next words you read:

Dear Abby:

I am doing fine. It feels funny to be talking and having somebody write down what you're saying. But I want to assure you that I am well. The great thing about not being able to use your hands is having people wait on you all the time. I may get spoiled and expect this same treatment when I get home. Home. I can't wait to see you and Darcy again. I can imagine how hard it must have been for you while I was missing in action. But everything is fine now. Please don't worry about me. I'll be home before you know it. I can't wait to see you again. Please tell Darcy how much I have thought about her, how I want to watch her grow up into the beautiful young lady I know she will be. I love you both very much.

It's me again, Fred Marcancio, Mrs. Webster. I want you to know that Bill is being awarded the Purple Heart and is being recommended for commendation for his heroism in the line of duty. Before he was wounded, he assisted, while under fire, a fellow soldier who had been pinned under falling debris, setting him free and no doubt saving his life. You have a right to be proud of your husband. Men like him are the reason that we are winning this terrible war.

The official notification from the Department of War stated that Technical Sgt. William J. Webster was reported safe on October 11th. That was the day Sister Angela offered her prayers for my father in the courtyard of St. Jude's Convent.

The bells rang out gloriously on the crisp winter air as I returned with groceries from Lucier's Meat Market on Christmas Eve. Although the war was not over, the priests of St. Jude had made an exception for the holiday, I thought, as I made my way over the icy sidewalk. At the corner of Mechanic and Third I paused, basking in the pealing of the bells. Although wartime had banished public displays of Christmas lights in Frenchtown, Christmas trees at tenement windows glowed red and green.

I was eager to arrive home, where my father and

mother and our own Christmas tree waited, but the singing of the bells caught and held me. Ascending in cascades, such joyous tumbles of sound, so joyous that I raised my face to the night, saw stars dancing in the sky as if in cadence to the bells, and I seemed to be floating above the pavement. Crazy thought, of course, but I smiled, content and happy. Christmas Eve and my father home and our family together again and now the glory of the bells, their *tintinnabulation*, remembering the Edgar Allan Poe poem we had read in school and that wondrous word, *tintinnabulation*, leaping to life even as the sound of the bells began to diminish.

I headed homeward, the ringing and the pealing growing fainter, then fading, the way colors fade, until, as I turned into our street, the night sky was silent again. Yet the bells still rang in my ears, sweet now in retrospect, as I reached our doorstep.

I started up the first-floor steps but stopped before placing my foot on the piazza, startled by a figure, like a shadow, standing in the corner. Frozen suddenly with fright, as well as with the cold, I was unable to cry out.

The shadow stepped forward.

"Darcy, it's me."

The streetlight struck the figure, and for a moment I was puzzled, although no longer frightened.

"Is that you, John Francis?" I cried out. He was in

an army uniform, the heavy overcoat too big for his slender frame, his thin, old-man's face pale and lost under the visored hat. "You almost scared me to death. What are you doing out here in the cold? Come on up, come inside."

"No," he said. "I can't stay. I have to get back to Delta, and the bus leaves in a few minutes."

Soldiers were always leaving in a hurry.

The wind rose, and we stepped deeper into the piazza near the LeBlancs' kitchen window for protection. "What are you doing in the army?" I asked. "You're too young—"

"I lied about my age," he said. "I have to go, Darcy. I have to do my part."

"Where have you been all this time?" I asked. "You and Kathleen Mary and your mother and father, all of you?"

"We split up," he said. "My father went crazy here that last night, and they took him away. To jail in Worcester. We all went to Lowell for a few days, then they split us up, my brothers to an orphanage, and me to an old uncle and aunt in Boston. Uncle Bim and Aunt Shirley."

He had not mentioned Kathleen Mary, and I waited for him to tell me about her, my anger returning as I thought of how she had not gotten in touch with me during all the time she had been away.

"I was lucky," John Francis said. "Uncle Bim and Aunt Shirley are old and they never had children and they treat me like their own son. But I had to get into the war. Before it's over. I know they felt bad, but I had to go."

But what about Kathleen Mary?

A gust of wind assaulted the piazza, and he stamped his feet, and I clutched the grocery bag to my chest.

"What about Kathleen Mary?" I said at last, afraid he might suddenly leave without telling me anything about her.

He drew back into the deeper shadows.

"She's dead, Darcy," he said. I could not see his face, but puffs of steam came out of his mouth, as if the terrible words were made visible.

I turned away, felt the grocery bag slip from my fingers and fall to the floor with a dull thud. I did not stoop to pick it up. There were a dozen eggs in the bag, and I didn't care if they were broken.

"How did she die?" I asked. My voice sounded far away, like someone else's voice.

"Pa didn't stay in jail long," he said. "He followed Ma and the other kids to Lowell. He was full of the drink and started after Kathleen Mary. She ran out of the house, and a car hit her. I wasn't even there."

I stood still, but something inside of me shifted,

something deep, subterranean, cold like a glacier, icy, colder than that December night.

"She didn't suffer, Darcy," he said, his voice hurrying. "They said she never came to after the car hit her. She died in the hospital without opening her eyes." Then, his voice flat: "She always said I was her protector, but I couldn't protect her from the worst thing of all."

"All this time I've been mad at her," I said. "Because she went away like that, because she never wrote to me."

"She felt bad about leaving like that," John Francis said. "She was going to write. She was going to send you a souvenir. I was with her when she bought it at the five-and-ten. In Lowell, before I went to Boston."

He fumbled with his overcoat, hampered by his gloves, hands loosening the brass buttons, then reaching inside. My own breath was like smoke coming from my mouth, and my feet were cold, but not as cold as that place deep in my body.

He drew out a small package and offered it to me. Not a package actually, but something wrapped in white tissue paper. I hesitated, then drew off my mittens and stuck them in my coat pocket. I wanted to touch with my hands whatever Kathleen Mary had touched with hers.

129

I took it from John Francis and unwrapped it, my fingers quickly stiff and cold, and stepped into the light to see it more clearly.

The merry movie eyes of Shirley Temple looked up at me. A miniature doll. Shirley Temple in a red-and-black kilt. Dimples in her cheeks. A ribbon in her hair.

"She said she made you give away your Shirley Temple stuff and always felt bad about that," John Francis said, stamping his feet and clapping his hands to keep the cold away. "When she died, I made a promise to myself that I'd bring it to you someday."

"Thank you, John Francis," I said, cradling the doll in my hand, holding it delicately but tightly so that it would not drop from my stiff fingers. "Please, John Francis," I said. "Please come into the house. My mother will fix you some hot cocoa."

How could I speak of hot cocoa with Kathleen Mary dead?

Shaking his head, he said, "I've got to go, Darcy. I'm not exactly on a pass. We're shipping out tomorrow, going overseas, and my sergeant let me come because he's a good guy. I don't want to get him into trouble. I figured this might be my only chance to see you."

"Kathleen Mary was my best friend," I said. "I'll never have a best friend like her again."

"She said that if she could be anybody in the

world, she would be you, Darcy." He clapped his hands together again and buttoned his overcoat and arranged his hat at a sharp angle on his head. I wanted to kiss his old-man's face, but only stood there. "I've got to go," he said.

"Thank you, John Francis," I said. "Thank you for coming. For bringing me this."

He saluted, like a real soldier, and I realized that John Francis O'Hara *was* a real soldier, even in the uniform that was too big for him.

Starting down the steps, he paused and called back, "Merry Christmas, Darcy."

"Merry Christmas, John Francis," I answered. "I hope you'll be safe, wherever they send you."

He went off into the night, his feet crunching on the snow, his figure silhouetted against the streetlight. "I'll pray for you," I called.

As he turned and waved, disappearing into the darkness, the bells began to ring again, but distant this time, barely audible, faint echoes of those earlier, glorious bells. I waited, listening, until the sounds died away. Then the wind rose, biting my cheeks, and I picked up the groceries and hurried across the piazza, into the hallway, and up the back stairs to our tenement.

My father's face had changed, from thin to gaunt, as if a sculptor had hollowed out his cheeks. His eyes were merry, however, with no hint of the old wistfulness. His arms were not bandaged, but he held them awkwardly, and stared at them sometimes as if they belonged to someone else.

He rose when I walked in, smiling, glad to see me, and then frowned: "What's the matter?"

"Nothing," I said, unable to speak about Kathleen Mary. "It's cold out," I said, putting down the groceries—the eggs had not broken after all—conscious of the Shirley Temple doll tucked away in my pocket. "When will we open the gifts?" I asked to deflect his attention, because Christmas gifts were meaningless now. "After supper?"

"Maybe we should wait until tomorrow morning, like normal people," he teased. I had earlier convinced him and my mother that the gifts should be opened on Christmas Eve instead of Christmas morning.

The aromas of the holiday filled the tenement—pine from the decorated tree in the corner of the living room, candles burning on the dining room table, my mother's fancy cookies baking in the oven.

She served us supper, all my favorites, hamburg, mashed potatoes and peas, which I chewed endlessly without any taste. She kept touching her hair, patting stray wisps into place. She had worried that my father might feel betrayed when he saw her cropped hair. "You could dye your hair pink and he'd still be glad to see you," I had assured her. She studied me for a long moment, and then hugged me to her. "You always say the right thing to cheer me up, Darcy." I felt suddenly older and nearer to her.

My father's homecoming was like the final scene in a movie at the Plymouth, except for the absence of background music. My mother and I had been watching at the window, waiting to see him come striding along Second Street, his duffel bag slung over his shoulder. At the last minute our vigil was interrupted by a pot boiling over on the stove. While we were in the kitchen, we heard footsteps bounding up the back stairs, and suddenly he was at the door, flinging it open, a splendid figure in khaki, all brass buttons and bright ribbons of valor on his uniform. My mother rushed into his open arms, and I watched them embracing, feeling safe and secure again, the way it had been when I was younger and my father would tease my mother—*I've got the time if you've got the place.*

But now Kathleen Mary was dead.

Before the dishes were washed and dried, Mr. and Mrs. LeBlanc arrived from downstairs, bringing us a *tourtière,* the meat pie that the French Canadians baked for holidays. My father gave me a look of sympathy: the opening of gifts would have to be postponed until they left. He had misinterpreted the sadness on my face. Mr. LeBlanc was talkative as usual, while his wife remained mute, smiling pleasantly.

He tried to teach me how to pronounce *tourtière*. He spoke the word carefully, *tourrr . . . tee . . . airrre,* rolling his *r*'s dramatically. My pronunciation was a pale imitation. Everyone laughed and I laughed, too, finding out for the first time how close laughing could be to weeping.

The fire in the stove warmed the kitchen, and Mr. LeBlanc began a long story about the old days in Canada when gifts were opened on Epiphany, the twelfth day after Christmas, and how the bells would ring throughout the parishes of the province.

"Wait till you hear our St. Jude bells," he said, "when the war is finally over." Turning to me: "You will love them, Darcy. Every child should grow up with church bells ringing in the ears."

"But I heard them tonight," I said. Remembering their glorious sound: "They are beautiful."

He looked puzzled. "What bells did you hear?"

"The church bells. They rang when I was on my way home from Lucier's."

Laughing again, his bald head gleaming, he said, "Poor Darcy. You hear things? In your head?" Curling his sentences, leaving question marks at the end of them.

"Not in my head, Mr. LeBlanc. My ears. I

stopped at the corner of Fifth and Mechanic and listened—"

"What time was this?"

"The market closed at six, and I left there just as Mr. Lucier was taking off his apron—"

"But I was in the church at six o'clock," he said. "To light some candles. And I heard no bells."

Their eyes were fastened on me. Had the color left my cheeks?

"Maybe it was the wind," my mother said. "Carrying the sound of music from downtown. The Christmas chimes they play for the shoppers."

"Or maybe music on a phonograph from one of the tenements," Mr. LeBlanc suggested while his wife nodded eagerly.

My father leaned forward and touched my shoulder.

"Or some other bells," he said.

So many miracles every day, Sister Angela had said. *Who can count them?*

"Yes," I said to my father. "Some other bells."

Later, after Mr. and Mrs. LeBlanc had said their good-byes and went back downstairs, I waited in the bedroom while my father and mother placed the wrapped gifts under the tree. "Don't come out until we call you," my father had cautioned, delight in his voice.

I took the Shirley Temple doll from the top of

the bureau and held it in my hands, caressing the porcelain cheeks, touching the eternal smile.

We'll find other bells to ring, Darcy, Kathleen Mary had said. *I will not desert you. That's a promise.*

Oh, Kathleen Mary.

I stood there in the bedroom holding my childhood in my hands. When my father called to me, I said good-bye to that lost childhood and went into the living room to open my Christmas gifts.

ABOUT THE AUTHOR

Robert Cormier, a former journalist, is the author of several brilliant and controversial novels for young people, which have won numerous awards. His books have been translated into many languages and consistently appear on the Best Books of the Year for Young Adults lists of the American Library Association, *The New York Times,* and *School Library Journal.* His most recent book for Delacorte Press was *Fade.*

Robert Cormier was born in Leominster, Massachusetts, and attended Fitchburg State College. In 1977 the college awarded him an honorary Doctor of Letters degree. He and his wife, Connie, live in Leominster. They have four grown children.

ABOUT THE ILLUSTRATOR

Deborah Kogan Ray is a painter and an illustrator who has received many awards for her illustrated children's books, including the 1987 Drexel Citation from Drexel University. Among the books she has written for children is *My Daddy Was a Soldier,* for which she drew upon childhood memories and talked to others who had lived through the Second World War.

Deborah Kogan Ray has two grown daughters and lives in Philadelphia.